GHOST OF A CHANCE

"Hey, hold on, what's the matter?" Aileen asked, grabbing me. "You look like you've seen a ghost."

"I did!" I sobbed. "I did see him. In the supermarket."

Aileen's mouth twitched in a smile. "A ghost in the supermarket? That's a new one."

"But I did see him! It's the boy from the old painting. I saw him twice at the house, and now he's followed me here. He's going to haunt me wherever I go," I cried. I looked back fearfully, then clutched at Aileen's arm. "Here he comes now," I whispered. "Tell me you see him, too!"

The figure in oils▒▒▒▒▒▒▒▒▒▒ boots was coming down th▒▒▒▒▒

Aileen ▒▒▒▒▒▒▒▒▒▒▒▒▒▒▒▒t ghost is Nat Fran▒▒▒▒▒▒▒▒▒▒▒▒▒▒▒gorgeous."

Ghost Of A Chance

Janet Quin-Harkin

BANTAM BOOKS
TORONTO · NEW YORK · LONDON · SYDNEY

RL 6, IL age 11 and up

GHOST OF A CHANCE
A Bantam Book / January 1984

Sweet Dreams and its associated logo are registered trademarks of Bantam Books, Inc. Registered in U.S. Patent and Trademark Office and elsewhere.

Cover photo by Pat Hill

All rights reserved.
Copyright © 1983 by Janet Quin-Harkin and Cloverdale Press Inc.
This book may not be reproduced in whole or in part, by mimeograph or any other means, without permission.
For information address: Bantam Books, Inc.

ISBN 0-553-23939-2

Published simultaneously in the United States and Canada

Bantam Books are published by Bantam Books, Inc. Its trademark, consisting of the words "Bantam Books" and the portrayal of a rooster, is Registered in U.S. Patent and Trademark Office and in other countries. Marca Registrada. Bantam Books, Inc., 666 Fifth Avenue, New York, New York 10103.

PRINTED IN THE UNITED STATES OF AMERICA

O   0 9 8 7 6 5 4 3 2 1

Ghost
Of A Chance

Chapter One

It's funny how days that are going to change your life start like any other day. Mine had started with an argument between my older sister, Kelly, and me over who was going to get to finish the Sugar Puffs and who would be stuck with the Wheaties. In spite of Kelly's constantly telling me about the strict diet she was on, she managed to wrestle the Sugar Puffs away from me.

"I need them more than you," she said, triumphantly pouring them into her bowl. "I have to develop strength for my job!"

Kelly had just been hired as a lifeguard the week before, and she was making me sick by parading around the house in her new red-and-white swimsuit and blowing her whistle at me.

"In that case, I'd think you'd need the Breakfast of Champions," I snapped at her. "All that sugar will give you a letdown just when you dive in to rescue the gorgeous drowning football player!"

Who knows where that fight would have ended if my mom hadn't come downstairs from her bedroom and my brother Steve hadn't walked in with the morning mail just then.

"Another letter from your crazy sister," Steve said to Mom, handing her a thick white envelope as he headed over to the refrigerator.

"She is not crazy," Mom said. "I won't have you talking that way about your Aunt Harriet. She may be a little weird, but she certainly isn't crazy."

Aunt Harriet was something of a family legend. She was much older than Mom and had always lived alone. She always kept an apartment in New York City, but would move to remote parts of the country for short periods. She dressed in Salvation Army rejects. And she made her living by writing Gothic novels of the most dramatic kind—you know the type of thing—girls in long, flowing nightgowns with windswept hair, standing in front of dark houses full of terrible secrets.

Mom had torn the letter open and was reading it. She had a concerned look on her face.

"Well, don't keep us in suspense any longer," Steve said through a mouthful of English muffin. "What crazy thing is she doing this time—living on wild rice or standing on her head or—"

"Oh dear, that's awful," Mom said.

We all looked at her. Even Kelly stopped munching her Sugar Puffs.

"Aunt Harriet's fallen down some stairs and broken her leg," said Mom.

"That's crazy enough," Steve said, grinning. Mom frowned, and Steve left the room in a hurry.

"Is she in the hospital?" Kelly asked.

"She is right now," Mom said, scanning the letter, "but she's going to be out at the end of the week, and she says she doesn't know how she'll manage in the big old house she's rented. It's full of stairs, she says here, and the nearest store is down a big hill and a mile away, and she doesn't have a car."

"So, what will she do?" Kelly asked. "She's not coming here, is she? I really don't want to give up my room again."

Mom smiled. "She says quite clearly that nothing, not even a broken leg, would make her spend a summer in Chicago—but she won-

3

ders if I could spare one of my girls for the summer to go to Maine," Mom said.

"Not me," Kelly and I said at the same time.

"It can't be me," Kelly wailed. "I've got my job, remember? I've been trying for years to get a lifeguard's job, and now I've finally got it. Meredith will have to go."

"I have plans, too," I said hotly.

"Like what?" Kelly asked.

"Things Peter and I are going to do."

"Oh, yeah, you and Peter—big deal!" Kelly said.

"You're just jealous because you don't have a boyfriend right now."

"Girls, girls," Mom said, then sighed. "Fighting won't help. I realize that neither of you wants to go, but it does look as if it had better be Meredith. After all, Kelly does have a job all arranged for the summer—"

"I might get a job, too," I said. "I was planning to start looking."

"Who'd hire a little shrimp of sixteen?" Kelly asked, giving me a triumphant leer.

"I'd rather be a mature sixteen-year-old than an immature seventeen-year-old."

"Girls, please!" Mom said a little more firmly.

"But, Mom!" I pleaded. "You can't do this to me! You know I've waited all my life for a real boyfriend. I never dreamed I'd ever meet anyone as great as Peter, and if I go away now, I'll lose him—I know I will!"

"I don't want to banish you for life, honey," Mom said, smiling. "It's only for the summer, and it may not even be the whole summer. Just until Aunt Harriet can get on her feet again. If your Peter is the right sort of boy for you, he'll wait that long."

I knew, actually, that Mom didn't think Peter was the right sort of boy for me. He drove a fast red sports car, which made him "unreliable" in her eyes, and she thought that I was getting in with a "bad crowd"—which wasn't at all true. They were just kids, like me, who wanted to have a good time. We liked to dance to loud music and party a lot, and, to tell the truth, I could never get over my luck at becoming a part of the group.

And then there was Peter himself—gorgeous blond Peter Borden with his halo of wiry curls and that fabulous smile of his. All the girls in school wanted to date Peter. I still couldn't believe that out of all those girls he had chosen me!

A couple of months before school had ended, we were paired off together to do an after-school project for our local clinic on smoking and lung disease. We had to spend a lot of time together interviewing people and making charts of statistics. One evening after working together, we stopped off for a pizza and had a good laugh about the woman we had just interviewed. Then before I knew it, Peter had asked me to a movie. We had been going out ever since.

And now I was going to be parted from him for the whole summer! It didn't matter how I pleaded or sulked, Mom had made up her mind. "At your age I would have been thrilled to see more of the world," Mom said. "A chance to take a free trip to Maine is something most girls would jump at. It will be very good for you. You need a chance to do new things and have new experiences."

The trouble was that I didn't want new experiences, not of the kind that Mom meant, anyway. I was perfectly happy in our nice, neat Chicago suburb with its matching houses and trimmed front lawns and the big shopping mall only a ten-minute walk away. An old, rickety house on the coast of Maine did not sound like my idea of fun. Later that day when Dad came home, I tried to explain to him that I was a "people person" and that I would shrivel up and die if I was stuck miles from civilization. He was usually on my side, but that time he sided with Mom and said the change would be good for me.

So I was condemned to the trip. Kelly walked around the house that evening looking smug and blowing her whistle for practice. As I watched her, I felt myself getting madder and madder. Life just wasn't fair. Kelly had been playing Miss Goody Two-Shoes since we were little kids; with her angelic face she always managed to get her own way. "What a sweet child," everyone always said about her, while I was usually described as a "handful!" (And no words could ever be found to describe Steve!)

I wasn't the only one who had bad feelings. She was jealous that I had grown to five feet seven inches, while she was stuck at five three. She also envied me my slim figure, which I didn't have to diet to keep. Also, my light brown hair had natural blond highlights, while Kelly needed to apply all sorts of Miss Clairol type of gunk to hers to turn it anything but mouse brown. But, actually, the bad feelings between us never lasted for too long, and even when we were angry with each other, the anger never ran *too* deep.

On the whole, I'd say we were a pretty loving family. I guess we were about average in the amount of fights we had. Once in a while I really appreciated my brother and sister— like all those times before I got my driver's license when Kelly would drive me anywhere, and the times Steve introduced me to his football player friends. And at that moment, faced with three long months of separation, I knew I would rather face Kelly and Steve at their most annoying than Aunt Harriet. Short of running away for the summer, there was no way I could get out of going to Maine. And running away, obviously, wasn't an idea I'd taken seriously.

"What sort of best friend are you, anyway?" I asked Marnie Hirsh, who came over two days later to help me pack. "If you were really my best friend, you'd hide me in the attic at your house for the summer. You've read *The Diary of Anne Frank*—you'd know how to do it. Instead of helping me out, you're forcing me to have an awful summer with an old witch."

Marnie laughed and pushed her glasses up on her nose. Marnie's glasses had been slipping down her nose since I had met her in kindergarten. She was always pushing them up.

"It might be fun," Marnie said wistfully. "Better than staying here and getting too hot and being too tired to walk down to the rec center for a swim. Just think of that gorgeous blue ocean and all those seabirds and lobsters and sailboats."

"*You* go then, if you think it'll be so wonderful," I snapped. "I'm sure Aunt Harriet doesn't care who takes care of her. But I warn you," I added with a laugh, "she's not exactly normal. In fact, when I was little, I used to think she was a witch. She writes Gothic novels, and she has this way of staring at you with those little beady eyes of hers—it gives you the creeps."

"In that case I'll stay right here," Marnie said. "I have to do some research for a paper, anyway."

Marnie was a genius. She always got straight A's and was definitely headed for Harvard or someplace like it.

"Well, the least you can do is keep an eye on Peter for me," I said as I packed a fourth pair of jeans into my suitcase. "You know—make sure he doesn't look at any other girls or anything."

"I will personally blindfold him for the summer," she said. "But you don't have to worry, Meredith. He's crazy about you."

"I wish I could believe that," I said. "A thousand miles is a long way away."

I tried to shut my suitcase. "Here, sit on this, will you?" I asked Marnie. "It won't shut."

Marnie shook her head. "It wouldn't matter if an elephant sat on it, it still wouldn't shut. You have too many clothes in it. Honestly, Meredith, you have enough packed to give a one-woman fashion show every day of the summer."

But I was not going to give up my clothes for anything. Apart from Peter, my major interest in life was clothes. In fact, the night before, I overheard my mother saying to my father, "I can't tell you how glad I am that she'll have a summer away from here. She is not at all motivated. All she thinks about these days are her clothes and her hair and this Peter."

Isn't that just typical! For years she had been bugging me about the way I looked, and now that I finally did care about my appearance, she started worrying about that! Seems like you can never satisfy a parent whatever you do.

Anyway, by the next morning my suitcases, still bulging, were finally shut. Marnie came over to the house at the crack of dawn to see me off, which was a pretty nice gesture since she likes to sleep late. I must admit that when I got into the car with Mom and Dad to drive to the airport, I couldn't help but feel just a teeny bit excited. I had only been on a plane a couple of times before, and those flights had been short ones when I visited Grandma in Minneapolis with the rest of the family. I had never flown a thousand miles, and I had never flown alone.

"Have fun," Kelly said in her purring voice.

"Write to me," Marnie yelled, waving like crazy as the car pulled away.

"Watch out Aunt Harriet doesn't turn you into a toad," Steve called, making horrible faces.

"I hope we know what we're doing," I heard my father say to my mother as we stood at the check-in counter. "After all, she is only sixteen. It's a long way to travel alone."

Suddenly I felt very important and grown-up. Of course I could handle it. I was mature and capable, and I didn't panic.

When the flight attendant asked me if I was coming home from college, I felt that I could handle anything!

Chapter Two

"Stormhaven?" asked the old man as he wiped the rain from his face. "The old Franklin place, you mean? Why would anybody want to go to Stormhaven at this time of night?"

The wind and rain blowing in my face made it impossible for me to answer that Stormhaven was the last place in the world I wanted to go to—that night or any night. But I didn't want to stay at that little bus station, either. I'd had a long ride from the airport.

"My aunt's renting it," I yelled at him, trying to speak above the storm. "I've come to look after her. Is there a bus or taxi or something?"

"Oh, yes," said the old man, not hurrying in the least, although the wind was blowing harder now and the rain was falling in torrents. "I recall now. Someone did rent it for the summer. Been empty for years before that. Couldn't find anyone to take it, on account of—" He broke off suddenly and checked himself. "On account of its being so cut off, that is."

"So, how am I supposed to get there?" I yelled. "Is it far?"

"Pretty fair way, especially in the dark," he said. Visions of my staggering over cliffs clutching my matching Samsonite luggage flashed before my eyes.

"And there's no taxi or anything?" I asked desperately.

"Sure, there's a taxi," he said. "It's over there." He jerked his thumb toward an ancient-looking car with old-fashioned fins in the rear. "And I'm the driver." Then he just stood there.

"Well, could you drive me, then?" I asked impatiently.

"I guess so," he said.

Then he turned his back on me and walked ahead to his car, leaving me to carry my own bags. After a few half-hearted coughs, the car's engine turned over, and we drove away from the station down the one street that made up beautiful downtown Rockville. The rain was pouring onto the windshield, and because the windshield wipers weren't working very well, I couldn't see much. We did pass a red neon sign, Ed's Grocery—Live Bait, and another, The Anchorage, which might have been the name of a restaurant or bar. But apart from those two lit-up signs, all I could make out were the dark shapes of low buildings. And then, suddenly, there was nothing. The road started to twist and turn, and I had to grab the armrest on the door to stop myself from sliding into the driver. He sat still, staring straight ahead, as if there were no one else in the car. He hadn't said a word since we started. I thought that maybe he was being polite and waiting for me to speak first or that maybe he was shy.

"Terrible weather, isn't it?" I said. "Is it as bad as this often in the summer?"

"Nope," he answered simply.

We lapsed back into silence. Great, I thought. If everyone is this friendly, I'm in for a great summer!

Which got me thinking about the summer I was missing at home. Was it only that morning that I had sat in our kitchen in Chicago, pouring syrup on waffles? It seemed like a lifetime ago. Now I was sitting in a cold, wet taxi half a world away, driving through a dark and stormy night toward a summer with an old, weird aunt I hardly knew. I guessed it was one of the wonderful new experiences Mom had been talking about!

My wandering thoughts were brought back to Maine when the old man sitting next to me began to speak. "This is nothing," he said. "You should see it when it's really fierce."

For a moment I had no idea what he was talking about. Then I realized he must be continuing our conversation about the weather. Some snappy dialogue! But at least he was talking. That encouraged me to ask, "Are we nearly there yet?"

Again he didn't answer, just stared straight ahead of him through the gloom. Then suddenly he pointed dramatically. "There it is," he said. "That's Stormhaven."

Chapter Three

The car lurched to a halt. I paid the old man, then opened the door. I was almost knocked down by the force of the wind and rain. The old man didn't offer to help, so I dragged my suitcases out from the backseat. Then I looked around. Surrounding me on all sides was unbroken blackness. I could hear the roar of breakers, pretty close by, crashing onto rocks and retreating. The wind was moaning through unseen trees that creaked and groaned in the storm. It seemed as if the whole night were alive and tormented.

For a moment I stood there, bewildered, not knowing what to do next. Then I heard the car engine start up again, and I sprang to life, grabbing at the door handle.

"Don't leave!" I shouted, pulling the front

door on the passenger side open. "I don't know where I'm supposed to go! Where's the house? I can't see anything."

The old man watched my display of emotion with a complete lack of interest. "It's up," he said. "At the cliff top. Just follow the steps and keep going up. You'll come to it."

Then he pulled the door shut, revved the engine, and drove away, leaving me alone in the blackness. I tried to fight my rising panic.

Be sensible, Meredith—look for the steps and follow them just like he said. But I couldn't be sensible. I had thought I was mature and sophisticated and could get along pretty well on my own, but now all I wished for were my parents standing right beside me and Dad saying, "Here, take my hand, it's dark," and Mom saying, "I'll make you a nice hot drink before you go to bed."

Oh, why do you have to be so far away? I thought. Why couldn't you be here? I still need you.

But they weren't here. "OK," I said to myself, "since there is no way back into town except by walking and since I'm getting wetter and colder every minute, the logical thing to do is to find those steps and get up to the house." I was proud of that speech, and immediately I began to move slowly until my foot stumbled against a step. Having found the bottom one, I could see the rest, a little lighter in color than the surrounding ground; they disappeared up the hill like a pale snake.

I bravely staggered upward, carrying my suitcases, but after a few steps, I gave in and put one suitcase down. The wind was so strong that I needed to hold onto the railing, and my luggage was just too bulky and heavy to carry with one hand. I remembered how Mom and Marnie had tried to persuade me to leave behind half of my stuff, and I now wished that I had listened to them. I had thought that twelve pairs of pants were necessary for survival. Now, I knew that they weren't.

I left the suitcase, stuffed with pants and everything else I had considered necessary, hidden in a clump of bushes and walked on up with only my overnight case. It was a good thing, too, because higher up the steps were uneven and crumbling, and for all I knew, there was a sheer drop to the ocean on one side of me.

Then, suddenly, the steps curved sharply to the right, and there was the house before me—a huge, black shape in the darkness of the night. No welcoming light streamed out from the windows. In fact, there was no sign of life at all.

Then I began to feel *really* scared. What if Aunt Harriet had already gone to bed? She wouldn't hear me knocking! What if she hadn't even been let out of the hospital yet? What if this were the wrong house? My head was buzzing with "what ifs" as I pulled up the heavy lion's head door knocker and brought it crashing down. Then, I waited.

There was silence, except for the noise of the ocean's pounding on the rocks. But when I had just about given up hope of anyone's coming to the door—it began to open slowly. Now I was absolutely terrified, and I stood shaking, unable to lift my feet to run; my heart was exploding in my chest. When an eerie, white face peered around the half-open door, I let out a terrible scream.

"Heavens, girl, you startled me," said a voice. "Don't yell like that."

Thank goodness, it was Aunt Harriet! I stepped closer to the door and looked in. There was my aunt, standing in the hallway, clutching a candle and looking like one of the apparitions who had visited Scrooge on Christmas Eve.

"Oh, Aunt Harriet, it's you," I said with relief.

"Well, who did you expect it to be—a ghost?" she asked.

"Nobody came to the door for so long," I said, "and then it opened so slowly."

"When one's leg is encased in plaster from thigh to toe, one hardly rushes to the door and flings it open," Aunt Harriet said dryly. "I can't move around much, dear child, which is why you are here. Now come inside, for heaven's sake."

"Now," she said when I was in the hall and the big door had been safely closed behind me, "come into the kitchen to warm up. What a night for you to arrive. If I had been expecting you, I would have gotten some supper ready."

"But didn't you get Mom's telegram telling you I was coming? She sent it right after we got your letter."

"Well, the telegram has to be brought to me, and service is not the most efficient here," Aunt Harriet said. "I expect you got here in the famous taxi, didn't you? Well, that old fool also delivers the telegrams. The only trouble is that he only does it when he feels like it. So, in this sort of weather . . ." She paused while I peeled off my wet jacket and brushed my hair back from my face. Then she pointed to a hook on the wall for me to hang the jacket on. "Well, Meredith, this really is a surprise!" she said. "I must say that I wasn't expecting you. I should have thought your mother would have sent Kelly, seeing that she is the eldest."

"Kelly has an important job this summer," I said bitterly.

"By the sound of it you weren't overjoyed to come and look after your old aunt," she said. "Well, I can't say that I blame you. There's not much to do here. That is, unless you like boating and that sort of thing." Then Aunt Harriet turned and hobbled, slowly and carefully down the long, dark hallway: her cast made a rhythmic clomp on the stone floor with every other step.

She opened a door and step-clomped into a big, old-fashioned kitchen. A gust of wind rushed to meet us and made the candles flicker alarmingly.

"Don't you have electricity here?" I asked, trying not to sound too nervous.

"Oh, the power's been cut temporarily," Aunt Harriet said calmly. "Every time the wind blows, the power lines come down. It happens so regularly that now I keep candles all over the house, just in case."

"Oh," I said, feeling very tired, depressed, and far from home. Aunt Harriet must have noticed because she said, "Sit down, Meredith, and I'll get you something nourishing to eat.

21

You look quite worn out. From Chicago to Maine is a long way for a young girl to come alone. In the morning you can tell me all about your adventures."

I sank into a chair, and in no time at all she put a bowl of some kind of strange-looking food in front of me.

"As I was saying," she went on, "if I'd known you were coming today, I'd have prepared you a proper supper, but this will have to do."

I took a big mouthful of whatever it was in the bowl, then tried not to spit it out. It was without doubt the most horrible thing I had ever eaten—crunchy, bitter, slimy, and cold all at the same time. When I finally managed to swallow it, I blurted out, "Aunt Harriet, what on earth is this stuff?"

"Just goat's milk yogurt with wheat germ," she said. "I no longer eat unwholesome foods. You'll find no processed food in this house, nothing with preservatives or additives. Nothing artificial—just pure, natural food."

That was about the last straw. I had put up with saying goodbye to my first real boyfriend, with a long, turbulent plane trip, a ride in the dark, the storm, the steps, and the candles; but the thought of three months without hamburgers and potato chips was more than I could bear.

"Aunt Harriet, I'm not really hungry. I'm just very tired," I murmured. "I think I'll go straight to bed. If you'll just tell me how to find my room . . ."

Five minutes later I was curled up like a little ball in the darkness, listening to the pounding of the surf below my window and the whine of the wind through the chimney tops.

Chapter Four

The first thing my eyes focused on in the morning was a young man. He was very good-looking, with dark hair and a neat little cleft in his chin. He looked down at me with eyes that seemed to be laughing straight into mine. He had a half smile on his face. I shot upright in bed, and only then did I realize that he was not real at all but only a large portrait on the wall across the room; its frame was hidden by drapes.

Even though I realized that it was just a picture, I couldn't stop staring at the subject. It was as if I were hypnotized by those eyes—eyes that were amber and flecked with brown. Wow, I wonder if there's anybody who's as good-looking as that in real life, I thought. I stared at him from my bed and suddenly real-

24

ized that he was a young man from long ago. He was dressed in a white shirt with a ruffle at the neck, and his hair was long and curled and tied back in a large black bow. In one hand he held a telescope as if he had just been looking out to sea; blue water glistened through the open window behind him.

Seeing the water in the painting brought me back to reality and reminded me of where I was. I got out of bed and walked across the room to the window. The floor was icy on my bare feet, and a draft came in through the cracks in the window frame. The sky was still gray and heavy with the promise of rain, and the wind was whipping up whitecaps on the ocean below. Suddenly I had a thought—that was the first time that I'd seen an ocean. Of course I had seen the Great Lakes plenty of times, and they *almost* counted, but this was a real ocean with waves rolling in from across thousands of miles. I tried to make myself feel excited, but I couldn't. If the ocean had looked blue and inviting, I might have felt different. But that day it looked cold and dangerous and not at all inviting. As I stood there at the window, I let my gaze wander— first down to the cliffs, then to the left and the right, where the rocky coastline faded into the sea's mist. It was a fierce scene, and I found myself longing for a friendly face. Even my sister's voice yelling at me up the stairs would have sounded good to me right then!

What didn't sound good was Aunt Harriet's voice calling from down the hall to me that it was time for us to make breakfast, and was I ever planning to get up that day?

I got dressed in a hurry, putting on the same clothes I had worn the day before—my suitcase was still hidden down below. I was fishing around in my makeup kit for my eyeliner when I realized how ridiculous I was being. There was nobody who could see me or care how I looked. What a depressing thought! I brushed my hair savagely. Then, even though the only person I was likely to see was Aunt Harriet, I found myself putting on a hint of green eye shadow and mascara. After all, everyone said my large brown eyes were my best feature, so I had gotten into the habit of making the most of those eyes.

A complete waste of time, I said to myself, looking critically at the finished product. What a shame that such beauty should be buried for a whole summer. I sighed, then grinned at myself—I wasn't a beauty and never would be, and I knew it!

"Off to my wheat germ and yogurt," I said out loud to my good-looking friend in the painting. "I hope you're thankful that you don't have to eat!" As I left the room, I could have sworn that he gave me a wink! Was it possible to have a crush on a painting?

Aunt Harriet was in her room, and I helped her down to the kitchen. In the cold light of morning I got the first good look at her I'd had in years, and it confirmed exactly what I had remembered: she was weird! She was tall and thin—I guess I take after her in height—with lots of gray, wispy hair escaping from bobby pins placed not too strategically all over her head. She had a long, thin face, too, with sunken eyes and a long, pointed nose. It was a clever face, and her eyes darted around as if they never missed anything. But it didn't look like the sort of face you'd want to be close to for too long. I had remembered that she dressed strangely. Today she was wearing a long, shapeless green skirt of heavy wool, which hung almost to her ankles and looked as if it had been inherited from the army, which had probably used it to cover a tank. Over the skirt Aunt Harriet wore a white embroidered blouse that looked Mexican, and around her shoulders was a black shawl with long, silky fringe. One leg was encased right down to the toes in heavy plaster and the other foot was wearing a rainbow-colored sock.

"I hope you slept well and the ocean didn't keep you awake too much," said Aunt Harriet. "People say that ocean noise is restful, but it kept me awake for a couple of weeks when I first came here. All that rumbling and crashing—not at all peaceful."

I told her that I had slept like a log, and she nodded as if I had done one thing right. "Then you'll be well rested and ready to start work," she said. "That's good. This wretched leg is such a nuisance to me. I haven't been able to touch the housework or do any shopping. It's impossible for me to get down that hill and into town. It's all I can do to stagger down the hall to my typewriter and back. You can get started after you explore a bit. You'll find the cleaning things in that closet in the hall. There's a vacuum cleaner you can use if we ever get our electricity back."

Great, I thought bitterly.

She started to limp across to the stove.

"That's all right, Aunt Harriet, don't fuss with anything. Sit down," I said bravely, "and tell me what you want done."

Luckily, she only wanted to boil some eggs. Even I could do that. I was so grateful that we weren't having wheat germ and yogurt for breakfast that I almost danced around the kitchen. Aunt Harriet told me that there were some hens at a nearby farm who laid eggs in a free-range setting. The eggs had no additives, preservatives, or hormones in them. That meant that she could eat them without getting poisoned, she explained matter-of-factly. I blessed those hens and really enjoyed the eggs, served with whole wheat bread and unsalted butter.

"The milkman brings me the eggs," Aunt Harriet said, "as well as anything else I particularly ask for. But he hasn't been here for the past few days because of the storm. I'm afraid we're rather isolated up here. Of course," she went on as I spread butter on my third slice of bread, "it was the isolation that attracted me here in the first place. The atmosphere is just right for my stories, don't you think?"

I didn't want to admit that I had never read any of her stories, so I just sort of nodded with my mouth full.

"But I must admit, living here does have disadvantages, especially since I don't have a car or a phone," she said.

"No phone?" I could put up with all sorts of inconveniences, but my life was centered around the phone. If I didn't spend at least an hour every evening talking to my friends, I got withdrawal symptoms. I had promised to phone Peter as soon as I arrived. The night before, I had been too exhausted to think about it. He would be wondering what had happened to me.

"Where is the nearest phone, then?" I asked. "I promised to call my boyfriend."

Aunt Harriet raised an eyebrow. "A boyfriend already? Not healthy at your age. I'm surprised that your mother allows it."

"He's very nice," I said hotly. "And what's more, I am sixteen, you know."

"Oh, quite an old lady," Aunt Harriet said with the ghost of a smile. "Well, the only phone is at the coffee shop in the motel in town. Some of the local fishermen hang out over there, and I'm sure they'll enjoy listening to your conversation."

On the wall behind my head a clock sang out "Cuckoo" loudly and rudely. Aunt Harriet struggled to her feet. "Well, this won't do," she said. "I had better get back to my writing, or I'll be behind schedule. I left Camilla trapped in the secret room, and I haven't figured out a way for Henry to rescue her yet. Why don't you explore the house a little, learn to find your way around—I'll meet you for lunch." Without waiting for me to say anything, she step-clomped out of the room. I could hear her cast slowly tapping its way down a long hall. Then a door shut far away in the house.

"Boy, is this ever going to be the worst summer experienced by a human being," I said to the empty room. "Nobody to talk to except *her*, and she makes fun of me, and I can't even call Peter or Marnie."

I began to feel terribly sorry for myself and very lonely. How was I going to survive without Marnie and Peter? I had never been out of phone contact with Marnie before. She was the sort of person who knew everything, and I was always calling her up to ask her the answer to a math problem or how to get the frizzies out of my hair or how to wash my angora sweater. . . . I realized guiltily that I hadn't phoned Marnie as often as I used to since I had met Peter. Marnie didn't have a boyfriend herself—boys were sort of scared by her braininess. I had been ignoring her. Peter and I hadn't wanted her tagging along as a threesome, and now I missed her badly.

Then there was Peter himself. I missed him so much that it hurt—a real, physical ache somewhere under my ribs. How could I survive for a whole summer without Peter? I remembered every detail of our goodbye scene: how he had kissed me and said, "Summer will be so boring without you. Who knows, I might get so desperate that I'll have to ask Marnie for a date."

"You could do a lot worse than Marnie," I said, jumping to the defense of my best friend. "She's one of the best people around."

"So you don't mind if I date her then?" he had said, teasing me.

"You have my permission to escort my best friend around if you want to," I said, "but you'd better not look at anyone else. Remember, Marnie will be keeping her eye on you for me, and she's going to write and tell me everything you do!"

I hadn't been worried then, but now, being miles and miles from Peter and having no telephone, I did worry a lot. A cute boy like Peter wouldn't wait the whole summer for me.

I was in the blackest mood as I wandered through the house. It was a spooky old place that went on endlessly, room after gloomy room with dark-paneled walls and high ceilings. I could see what Aunt Harriet meant in her letter to Mom about stairs everywhere. They went up to turret rooms, and down to little alcoves hidden behind heavy velvet drapes.

When I came to a room with a big bay window that jutted out over a little garden, I knelt on the window seat and looked out. The garden was surrounded by a high stone wall with an iron door in it. It was full of shrubs that, in spite of the protecting wall, were twisted and bent by the wind from the sea.

To the left I could just glimpse the road that wound down toward the town. The town itself was lost in the mist. It seemed a very long road, and I had depressing thoughts about walking all the way back with armfuls of groceries, or even going down to make a phone call.

I'd better make friends with someone who has a car, I thought. Maybe a cute guy! Then I decided that everybody in town was probably over seventy and just as grouchy as the old taxi driver.

Suddenly, a movement in the shrubbery caught my eye. A slim, dark-haired boy emerged, as if from nowhere, opened the iron door, and disappeared out through it. He looked strangely familiar, and I tried hard to remember where I had seen him before. Then I did remember and felt my skin prickle—it was the cute boy from the portrait in my room!

Chapter Five

Let me tell you right now that I don't believe in ghosts. I am a very sane, levelheaded sort of person. In fact, my family often used to tease me about being so sensible: "It's no use expecting Meredith to understand, she has no sense of adventure," they'd say, or, "Meredith never gets excited about things!"

So, if I didn't believe in ghosts, why did I think I had seen a gorgeous guy from a two-hundred-year-old painting walk across the garden and disappear? There must be a logical explanation, but at that moment I just couldn't think of it.

I did ask Aunt Harriet about it when I took her a cup of herb tea. "Aunt Harriet, is there a gardener or someone who works up here?"

"A gardener? Why do you ask—do you like gardening?"

"No, it's not that"—she wasn't going to get me pulling weeds on top of everything else—"it's just that I saw a strange young man in the garden just now."

"There's no gardener here," Aunt Harriet said. "I wonder who it could have been? The owner comes and takes care of the place every now and then. Apart from him, nobody comes here except for my milkman." She looked back at the piece of paper stuck in her typewriter. "Now, let me see, where was I—after Camilla screamed and the white hand came around the curtain . . ."

Then she was back tap-tapping away, and I was left with no explanation about my mystery figure. So I decided to retrieve my wet suitcase and unpack.

By that time it was raining hard again, and I really didn't look forward to walking down to town. I had almost made up my mind to go shopping, though, rather than have another supper of yogurt and wheat germ, when a horn honked in the parking area below the house, and there was the famous milk truck. I grabbed an umbrella and ran down to meet the milkman and was surprised to find out that "he" turned out to be a girl about my age with carrot red hair and so many freckles that her face looked like a giant Florida orange. The orange broke into a big, friendly grin when she saw me.

"I just honked to let the old lady know I was coming up. I was surprised to see someone come down the steps. You must be her niece—she said you might be coming."

I smiled back. "My aunt kept talking about the milkman, but I must say you are the funniest-looking man I've ever seen!" I said.

Her grin grew even wider. "I help my dad out during school vacation. He'd rather be out on his boat than working, and I can always use the money. My folks only buy me two pairs of jeans and two sweaters for school each year, and everyone knows that a girl can't survive on that."

I nodded sympathetically.

"My name's Aileen Kinney," she said. "What's yours?"

"Meredith Markham. And you don't know how glad I am to meet somebody my own age. I was scared that everyone around here would be over seventy."

Aileen smiled. "Most of them are. It's hard to get young people to stay up here because there's no work. I doubt I'll come back after college. I mean, it's just dead up here. No life at all. One or two dances a year over in Littlehampton and movies that are so old that everybody in them wears funny clothes, and all the boys in the audience always yell out rude, dumb things!"

"So there are some boys around here, then?" I asked hopefully. I knew I was going to be true to Peter, but that didn't stop me from wanting a few boys around, just for decoration.

"Oh, there really aren't too many good ones," she said, wrinkling her nose. "I usually date the summer visitors myself. The few boys there are around here just think about fishing, and they stink something terrible when they've been out in the boats gutting fish all day. Are you going with someone yourself?"

I sighed. "With the most terrific boy in the world. And now he's a thousand miles away."

"Boy, you must be a loving niece or a saint to come here and leave him," Aileen said.

"Actually I didn't get much choice," I said bitterly. "My mom volunteered me for the job. Next thing I knew I was on a plane."

"Sounds like my mom," Aileen said. "Bossy. Which reminds me—I'll get bawled out for sure if I don't show up back at the dairy pretty soon. Does your aunt need anything besides the milk and eggs?"

"What do you have?" I asked hopefully.

She pulled the hood of her bright yellow oilskin poncho over her head, jumped out of the truck, ran around to the back, and flung open the doors of the truck to reveal an Ali Baba's cave full of goodies.

"Wow," I said, my eyes lighting up hopefully. "I think I'd better stock up while she's busy typing. She doesn't believe in real food these days."

"So she tells me every time I see her," Aileen said. "Queer old thing, isn't she? I'm glad to see that you're normal."

"I am *very* normal," I said. "And one of the things I can't live without is junk food." While I spoke, I was already grabbing bags of potato chips, a package of hot dogs, ketchup, and a handful of Snickers bars.

"Now at least I won't starve before you come up here again," I said. "How often do you come by?"

"Oh, I try to get up here twice a week, but you can never tell. The weather's been so bad this year that my routes keep getting flooded or blocked by fallen trees. But you should come down to town. I'm at the dairy around lunchtime most days. We could go and have a soda together, and I'll show you all the sights and the few boys that are worth knowing."

Then she jumped back into her truck and drove off at a hair-raising speed down the hill. I felt a bit better as I climbed up to the house with my precious cargo of emergency rations. Now that I knew I had a friend in town and that I wasn't going to starve for a couple of days, I felt that I could face anything again.

It turned out that Aunt Harriet was so busy getting Camilla away from the white hand that she didn't want any lunch. So I had a great time in the kitchen cooking hot dogs and smothering them in ketchup. They tasted fantastic, and so did the potato chips dipped in ketchup and two of the Snickers bars. After I had cleaned away the telltale evidence of my eating orgy, I wondered what to do next. The big grandfather clock in the hall only said one o'clock. A glimpse through the window showed that the rain was still pouring down. So what was I going to do with a whole afternoon? Other than clean, of course. That could wait.

What would I do on a rainy summer afternoon at home? I wondered. The answer came to me immediately: play records with Peter, and if Peter was busy, I'd play chess with Marnie or just talk to her on the phone. Failing all else I'd watch a soap opera on TV and see who was married to whom on "General Hospital" that week.

A thorough check of the house confirmed my worst suspicions. Aunt Harriet definitely did not have a TV set. Withdrawal symptoms began to set in, my palms felt sweaty, my head began to throb—a whole summer without Alan Alda and "The Dukes of Hazzard." I didn't think I'd be able to make it.

"Shame on you, Meredith Markham," I said out loud. "You're lost without the comforts of civilization. If you haven't got your friends to talk to or your TV to watch, you don't know what to do." It came as quite a shock to me.

Maybe I should buy some paints when I get down to town and do some pictures of the seashore, I decided. I had always liked art in school, and everyone said I showed promise. But that didn't give me anything to do right then, at that moment.

In desperation I curled up on an ugly red velvet couch and picked up one of Aunt Harriet's books. *The Curse of the Falcon* it was called. I smiled at the cover: a woman with long black hair, wearing the usual white robe that revealed almost everything, was running away from a big, eerie-looking house while a figure on horseback watched on the horizon and a big black bird hovered in the air.

Just one great big cliché, I thought and idly flipped through the pages.

Unfortunately it fell open to the page where the wife finds out about her husband's madness and he then decides to poison her as he had poisoned his first wife. So, then I had to read on to find out if she'd drink the cup of poison or not. Next thing I knew I was hooked. I read nonstop until I finished the whole book in an hour. Then I went to look for more of Aunt Harriet's books.

Would you believe that Meredith Markham, who used to have to be forced to read a book for school and never read one outside school, actually got through two of Aunt Harriet's novels that afternoon?

After I finished the last book, I went in to Aunt Harriet's study to help her back to the kitchen for dinner. Her leg seemed to hurt her much more at the end of the day than in the morning, and I found her sitting at her desk, writing with her leg propped up on a coffee table. I looked at her and at the paper in the typewriter with new respect. We had always made fun of her books before, but now I realized that they couldn't be that bad if I had wanted to read two in one afternoon.

In fact, they had been exciting and scary! So scary that I still felt jumpy in the big, dark house.

"Goodness, is it supper time already?" Aunt Harriet asked pleasantly as I came in. "I had no idea. I'm not nearly so far along with this story as I wanted to be. Poor Camilla, I'd meant to have Doctor Stevenson arrive with the snake antivenom serum before I stopped tonight. Ah, well, it can't be helped."

While she spoke, I was busily reading the words in the typewriter. "What happens to her?"

She laughed. "Like all my public, you, young lady, will just have to wait and find out."

"Not fair, Aunt Harriet," I said. "Do you realize you've got me hooked on your books?"

"Well, at least that shows you've got good taste," she said. A grimace of pain passed her face as I eased her to her feet. "Stupid leg," she said. "I could be going for lovely, long walks along the seashore right now if it weren't for this leg."

"Not today you couldn't," I said. "It's blowing a gale out there."

"That's good walking weather," Aunt Harriet said. "I never miss my daily walk, whatever the weather. Now let's go and get dinner."

Together we made our way slowly down the

hall to the kitchen, Aunt Harriet leaning heavily on my arm. As we came into the kitchen, she sniffed suspiciously and looked around. "Strange smell," she said. "Smells like someone's been cooking hot dogs in this room."

"Hot dogs, Aunt Harriet?" I asked innocently. "What a strange idea."

"Very strange," she said. "You'd never find any repulsive, additive-stuffed junk like hot dogs in my house. I wonder what it was that smelled like them?" Aunt Harriet looked at me and laughed.

"I've no idea," I said, hastily kicking an empty potato chip bag under the refrigerator. "Now, what do you want me to prepare for dinner?"

After we finished eating our beans and rice, I started to wash the dishes, and Aunt Harriet took out a book.

"Now, where did I put my spectacles this time?" Aunt Harriet asked, poking through the clutter on the kitchen table. "Oh, I remember now. I left them in the study. Run and get them for me, Meredith, there's a dear."

I grabbed a candle and walked along the passage. The scenes in my aunt's books haunted me every step of the way—the panel that slides open to reveal the killer's hand, the snake that strikes from the darkness, the low moan from the locked room. . . .

That passageway seemed to go on forever, and the candlelight played odd tricks with the walls all the way to the study.

I am perfectly calm, I said to myself. But I wasn't. My heart was hammering so loudly that it seemed to outdo the tick of a grandfather clock. Finally I came to my aunt's study. The room was full of the moaning of the wind and the crash of breaking waves. I looked over toward the windows and watched the drapes stir with unseen breezes, making the shadows on the walls appear to move. After taking a deep breath, I tiptoed in silently, as if I didn't want anyone, or anything, to know I was there.

Aunt Harriet's glasses lay on the typing table. I picked them up quickly with a trembling hand.

"Mission accomplished," I said out loud.

As I turned back toward the door, I heard a sound, the sound of a door slowly closing down a set of stairs. I crept out of the room and peeked down the stairs into the darkness where the old storage rooms were. Surely Aunt Harriet couldn't have gone down there. So who was it? I stood at the head of the stairs and peered into the gloom, hardly daring to breathe. Then I heard the sound I hadn't wanted to hear—the slow, measured tread of footsteps below me. I cowered against the stairrail, too frightened to move or to scream. A flicker of light came along the passage below. It lit up a handsome face I had seen before—in a portrait in my room and once as it had disappeared in the garden.

Chapter Six

That night I found it impossible to get to sleep, even though Aunt Harriet had laughed at my seeing a ghost.

"But I saw him, Aunt Harriet! It was the boy from the portrait in my room, and he was carrying a candle—"

"What you saw was probably one of the fishermen sent by the owner into the storeroom. Some of them store their fishing stuff up here, and there's a way up from the beach."

"But he didn't look like a fisherman. He looked like—someone from long ago, like a ghost. It was horrible!"

When Aunt Harriet found that she couldn't calm my hysterics or get me to sleep in the room with the picture, she let me make up a rollaway bed in her room, where I finally drifted off into an uneasy sleep.

The next morning I woke to find the sun streaming in through the window. I got up and looked out. The sea sparkled, and the view was like something from a picture post-card. It felt like quite a different world, and I realized how dumb I had been the previous night. It must have been all those books I had been reading.

Then I remembered that I had to call Peter. After all, he must be frantic with worry about me by then.

"I think I had better go down into town this morning," I said to Aunt Harriet as I stood at the stove, stirring her oatmeal. "It's about time I looked around a bit, and you said you needed some food from the store."

"Ah, yes," she said. "There are some things I want. But make sure you don't go to the supermarket. You'll find everything we need at the natural foods store across the street from it. They have very good quality foods, even organically grown vegetables. I'll write you a list."

The list she wrote was half a mile long, and I wondered how I was ever going to stagger up the hill with everything on it. But when I finally set out, it was such a beautiful day that nothing could make me feel down. The grass along the road was brilliant green and flecked with tiny blue flowers; sea gulls drifted lazily in the endless sky; and the air smelled of salt and seaweed.

I found myself skipping along like Dorothy in *The Wizard of Oz.* "I'm going to call Peter. I'm going to call Peter."

The town was not much more spectacular by day than it had been in the dark. There was still only one main street with a motel, The Tides—Color TV in All Rooms—Heated Pool, at one end and Ed's Grocery—Live Bait, at the other. In between were a police and fire station housed together in one tiny building with a fire truck parked out back, a souvenir store with some horribly tacky hats and plastic lighthouses in one window and some really nice craft items in the other. There was a small drugstore with plastic buckets and shovels in the window, then Aunt Harriet's favorite natural foods store, called The Good Earth. On the other side was the dairy, but there was no sign of Aileen or her truck.

I headed over to the motel to call Peter and found the telephone right away. I dialed the operator and gave her the number. Then I poured a whole handful of change into the phone, and waited. Two men who looked like fishermen came past and stared at me with interest, making me blush stupidly, as if I were about to make an obscene call. Still, I was very excited.

Come on, Peter, answer, I commanded him silently. I knew that his parents were at work and that he'd be the only one home.

Then finally the phone was picked up. "Hello?" came a sleepy voice at the other end of the line.

"Peter? It's Meredith."

"Oh—hi, Meredith!"

"Did I wake you?"

"Yeah, I guess you did."

"Serves you right for sleeping so late. I've been up for a couple of hours."

"Yeah, but it's an hour earlier here."

"Sorry, I forgot. How's things?"

"Pretty good. How's things with you?"

"Fine, I guess. Nothing to do up here."

"Nothing to do here, either. I may get a job. Marnie's dad thinks he knows of something. Marnie's looking, too. We're both broke, as usual."

"Tell her hi from me, will you?"

"Sure."

There was a pause. I was conscious of the two fishermen, hanging around the coffee shop, watching me. How could I say what I wanted when two strangers were listening in?

"I'm calling from a coffee shop in the town's only motel," I said. "We don't have a phone at the house. So I can't say anything personal. But I miss you already."

"I miss you, too," he said. "How's your old, weird aunt?"

"Pretty awful. She lives on goat's milk and alfalfa sprouts."

He laughed. "That'll keep you slim!" His laugh sounded wonderful and so close that I felt as if I could reach out and touch him.

"Peter—" I said. A loud beeping came on the line.

"Your three minutes are up," said a flat voice. "Please deposit forty cents for each additional minute."

I fished around in my wallet. I didn't have any more change.

"I have to go," I told Peter. "I'll try and phone you again. Write to me, OK?"

"Sure," he said. "If I get up the energy. You know what I'm like at writing. I can never get my school assignments done in time—letters are even worse."

"Well, bye," I said.

"Bye," he said.

The line went dead. I stood there for a while,

holding the phone in my hand before I put it back on the hook. Then I walked away, feeling as if I had just gotten some very bad news. Why did I feel so disappointed? I tried to figure it out: Peter had sounded pleased to hear from me—so why did I feel afraid? Was it that he hadn't told me how worried he'd been not to have heard from me? Was it that I'd had to say I missed him first? I didn't know. All I knew was that I felt uneasy, as if something terrible were about to happen.

I walked out into the sunlight and tried to tell myself that phone calls from motels are never easy, also that people are never at their best when they just wake up.

I wandered back down the street and went into the craft shop and bought myself a sketch pad and some watercolors. Then I got Aunt Harriet's natural foods, and finally, I went into Ed's Grocery to treat myself to some junk. Ed had quite a little supermarket, and I wandered up and down the aisles drooling at the displays of sour cream-and-onion-flavored potato chips, Twinkies, and Devil Dogs. The store was pretty packed; there were mothers with babies in shopping carts, tourists buying food for picnics, and fishermen buying bait. I walked past the cereals and stopped to wonder if I could smuggle in some Sugar Puffs for when I got tired of oatmeal. As I turned away from the cereals, a boy left the bait counter and came straight toward me. I looked at his face and felt my jaw drop as I started to scream. It was the ghost!

My scream caused panic in the narrow aisles. Mothers snatched up their kids. Someone yelled "Fire!" and someone else called out "Purse-snatcher!"

But I was only aware of all the commotion in the back of my mind. I turned and fled through the door, not noticing who I pushed out of the way. Outside I didn't stop running until I bumped into Aileen.

"Hey, hold on, what's the matter?" she asked, grabbing me. "You're as white as a sheet. You look like you've seen a ghost."

"I did." I sobbed. "I did see him. In the supermarket."

Aileen's mouth twitched in a smile. "A ghost in the supermarket? That's a new one."

"But I did see him! It's the boy from the old painting. I saw him twice at the house, and now he's followed me here. He's going to haunt me wherever I go," I cried. I looked back fearfully, then I clutched at Aileen's arm. "Here he comes now," I whispered. "Tell me you can see him, too!"

The figure in oilskins and big sea boots was coming down the street toward us.

Aileen turned and looked back. "I only see Nat Franklin," she said, "and he's no ghost."

Chapter Seven

My former ghost hurried up to us, his big boots slapping on the sidewalk. Now that I could look at him in daylight, I could see that there was nothing transparent about him. His dark hair was blown by the wind into untidy waves. His face was tanned, and his skin was wrinkled around his eyes into laugh lines. He looked like any perfectly ordinary boy, except that his amber eyes, flecked with brown, were the eyes in the painting on my wall.

"What happened?" he asked in an ordinary human voice. "Did someone snatch your purse?"

His face showed concern as he looked directly at me.

I tried to think of something to say that

wouldn't sound too stupid, but no words came.

"She's OK now," Aileen said. "She just had a bad fright."

"Are you staying at the motel?" he asked. "You'd better go and sit down somewhere. You look awfully pale."

Again Aileen answered for me. "She's staying up at Stormhaven with her aunt. I'm surprised you didn't know that."

His face crinkled into a smile. "Oh, yeah, I remember she said that one of her nieces was probably coming. I'm Nat Franklin. My family owns Stormhaven. We used to live there, but the energy bills were so enormous that we had a smaller house built closer to town. We rent out Stormhaven to visitors whenever we can now."

"Oh, so you own Stormhaven," I said, sounding like a parrot. I was remembering what my aunt had said . . . "The owner comes up here sometimes." The fright had worn off, and now I began to feel very dumb.

"How do you like the house?" Nat asked. "A monstrosity, isn't it? But we can't bring ourselves to tear it down or sell it. It's been in the family for two hundred years. My great-great-great-grandfather—I forget exactly how many greats—built it. They say he made a lot of money from smuggling. There's a passage that goes from the storerooms to a cave on the shore. Remind me to show it to you sometime. There's a big portrait of him in one of the bedrooms."

"I saw it," I said. "He looks just like you."

"That's what my mother always says," Nat said, grinning. "I can't see the resemblance myself. I'm much better looking!" he added, then laughed.

"Well, we can't stand around all day hearing about your wonderful family history, Nat Franklin," Aileen said. "Come with me, Meredith, and I'll give you a ride home in the truck."

I couldn't really refuse her. I turned to go.

"Bye, Meredith," Nat called after us. "Say hello to my great-great-great-grandfather for me!"

He turned away, waving a big hand at me. I still had to ask him the most important question.

"By the way, Nat," I asked, trying to sound casual, "did I see you up at the house last night and yesterday morning?"

"Me?" he said, trying to look innocent. "Why, I haven't been near the house in weeks. See you around." Then he walked away—rather hurriedly, I thought.

"What's the matter, Meredith?" Aileen asked as we were bumping along in the milk truck. "You look as if you've got something on your mind."

"Well, in a way I do," I said. "It's Nat Franklin. I swear he was the ghost I saw at the house twice. The first time he was moving quickly through the shrubbery as if he didn't want to be seen. The second time he was down in the basement storeroom creeping along carrying a candle. But he just told me he hasn't been near the house at all. Now, why would he lie? After all, it's his house. He has a perfect right to be there. It doesn't make sense."

Aileen shrugged her shoulders. "Who knows with Nat Franklin? You never know what he's up to."

"You mean you don't trust him?" I asked.

"I don't rightly know," Aileen said. "He doesn't go out with any of the girls around here, but he's friendly enough. Nobody really knows him too well."

"He *is* cute," I commented, remembering the way his tiger eyes smiled at me and thinking of the neat little cleft in his chin and the way that black, unruly hair waved across his forehead.

"Oh, he's cute all right," Aileen said. "But

don't get any ideas in that direction. He's already spoken for, as they say. I bet he could give a girl a good time if he wanted to. He never seems to be short of cash—though where it comes from, who knows?"

"Oh, you don't have to worry about me," I said. "I'm not interested for myself. I told you about my fantastic boyfriend at home, remember? I really don't want to look at anyone else."

But if that was true, why couldn't I stop thinking about Nat and his tiger eyes for the rest of the day?

Later, at the dinner table, I decided to get as much information about the Franklins as possible out of Aunt Harriet. I tried to figure out how to broach the subject tactfully while she put my dinner in front of me—a plateful of brown rice, bean curd, steamed, organically grown carrots, and soybean sprouts. I was just thinking that I might sell my soul for a Big Mac when she asked me about my day in town, which, of course, allowed me to bring up the topic of Nat.

"Aunt Harriet, what do you know about the Franklins?" I asked. "I met Nat Franklin in town today, and he started to tell me about his family history."

"Ah, the Franklins," Aunt Harriet said,

beaming. "They are a fascinating family. They started with a pirate turned respectable, so it's said. Or at least, semirespectable. They say that the first Franklin made money from smuggling, and there are hints that they kept up the smuggling until very recently. Of course, those are just local rumors. You know how people like to embroider stories for tourists. But there is a secret entrance to the cellars down below—it goes right down to the beach. Some people say the family used to be wreckers, too—you know—people who would lure ships onto rocks to steal their cargo. I don't suppose we'll ever know how much is real and how much is legend. The Franklins certainly aren't rich anymore. They couldn't afford to keep up this place, and they live in a small cottage they built over in the next bay. It's closer to town. Mr. Franklin runs a little restaurant on Main Street—The Anchorage, I think it's called."

She spooned another helping of bean curd onto her plate. "So you met Nat, did you? He's such a nice boy. I do enjoy it when he comes up here to visit. He's very interested in wildlife, you know. You should ask him to show you around a bit."

Nat Franklin, I thought afterward, you are getting more interesting by the minute! Two people had described him, and each of them saw him in quite a different way. To Aileen he was someone not to be trusted. To Aunt Harriet he was a nice boy interested in wildlife! Aileen said he had lots of money, and Aunt Harriet said his family wasn't rich anymore. And I—I had seen him twice in our house, and yet he claimed he hadn't been near the place. It didn't make sense, unless—unless Nat Franklin had taken up where his family left off. Could it be that he was a smuggler like his ancestors? That would explain why he had money when his family didn't, why he hadn't wanted to be seen at the house, and why he was creeping through the old store-rooms at night.

Suddenly the summer didn't look so boring anymore. I'm going to do some spying of my own, I thought. And I'm going to find out if he really is a smuggler!

Chapter Eight

Although I snooped around a lot during the next few days, I didn't manage to catch Nat at his smuggling. The weather got windy and rainy again, so I didn't even go back into town. Instead, I sat on the window seat and stared down the road, willing the mailman to bring me a letter from Peter. I was dying to write to him, but I felt that he was the one who should write first.

In the end, though, when four more days had passed and no letter came, I decided to write anyway. When I started the letter, there didn't seem much to say. The old house and the ghost and my search for the smuggler all sounded pretty dumb when I tried to put them down on paper. All my adventures in Maine were so far removed from suburban

Chicago and my life there that I knew Peter wouldn't understand. So I wound up writing, "Nothing much has happened—there isn't even a TV, and most of the time there's no electricity. And I've done a bit of reading, but not much else." I didn't even mention Nat. I finished up by saying that I missed Peter and hoped he would write. It was a wishy-washy sort of letter, and I hoped his to me would be much better.

When a letter finally arrived for me, it was from Marnie and not from Peter at all. She said that they had both gotten jobs at Hamburger Haven, a new place that opened up across the expressway. It was very hard work, and sometimes they didn't get home until midnight, but they had a lot of laughs. They finally had a day off the next day and were going on a picnic with the rest of the gang. Then she gave me bits of news about all our other friends: "Becky finally got her braces off and looks fantastic; Bob and Jennie are about to split up; Carrie got these beautiful black velvet jeans that would look great on you because you're so tall; and, oh, Peter says to tell you hi!" I had just finished reading the letter when Aileen arrived.

"Phew, what a day," she said, standing on the front porch and quickly shaking the rain from her enormous rain poncho. "If it goes on raining much more this summer, I'm going to start building myself an ark." She started to come in without waiting to be asked. "This delivery business is for the birds. Next summer I'll get myself a nice safe job in one of the stores, where I can stay warm and dry all day." She hung her poncho up on a hook near the door and turned to smile at me. "So, how's it going? You recovered from meeting your ghost yet?"

"I guess so," I said.

"Well, you don't sound too happy. Is it just the weather getting you down, or are you still being haunted?"

"Don't make fun of me," I said. "I really did think he was a ghost, and so would you if you saw him lurking in the shadows in your house with a candle late at night. You want a cup of coffee? I was just about to fix myself one." We started walking toward the kitchen.

"Sure," she said. "That might bring my frozen body back to life. But I didn't think your aunt went in for coffee."

"She doesn't. Only herb teas. But I bought myself a little jar of instant, and I make it when she's off in her study. We drink a lot of coffee at home, and I just can't make it on sassafras tea."

"I don't blame you," Aileen said, sinking onto one of the kitchen chairs.

"You know," I said, putting some water on to boil, "I do have to be careful to open the windows afterward. My aunt has a very keen nose that smells forbidden food a mile away. I've had to become a closet Snickers eater."

Aileen laughed. "Well, if things get too bad, you can always meet me down at the coffee shop at the motel, and we'll have a sinful hamburger together, smothered in ketchup."

"I'd like that," I said. "I miss having my friends around to talk to, although I'm not sure I've got any friends anymore."

"Bad news from home?" Aileen asked.

I eased into a chair across from her. "Pretty bad," I said. "I feel so powerless and far away."

"Boyfriend trouble?"

"I don't know, Aileen," I said, absentmindedly stirring three spoonfuls of honey into my coffee—Aunt Harriet never kept sugar in the house. "I really don't know, that's the problem. You see, I asked my best friend to keep an eye on my boyfriend for me—"

"And she's caught him cheating?"

"No, just the opposite. She's keeping a very good eye on him. They've got jobs together. She just wrote to me and said they were having a lot of laughs together. Now what on earth does that mean?"

"So you think she's after him herself?" Aileen asked.

"No, not really," I said. "She's a good friend. She wouldn't do a thing like that to me—and Peter would never—it's just—" I broke off and sighed, trying to put my thoughts into some sort of order. "It's just that I'm so far away, and they're having a good time without me. And I guess I'm disappointed that Peter hasn't written. I mean, what sort of a boyfriend is he if he can't even be bothered to write to me?"

"He may be busy with his job," Aileen said. "And some boys just aren't good at expressing themselves on paper."

"I suppose you're right," I said. "But it just doesn't seem fair. I had to come here when I didn't want to. If I could have stayed home, it would have been me working with Peter and having lots of laughs."

"I don't see what you're complaining about," Aileen said and grinned. "After all, none of your friends is being chased by a cute ghost. Have you seen any more of him, by the way?"

"Not a thing. I think he's staying far away

from crazy people like me. He hasn't been near the place since you and I saw him together in town."

The next morning I was wakened out of a deep sleep by a strange noise. The sky outside my window was barely streaked with light, and my watch said it was only just after five. I lay in my bed surrounded by the warm, comforting blankets, with my eyes wide open and listening. Then it came again—the sound of something heavy being dragged somewhere below my room.

I leaped out of bed, almost regretting it as my feet touched the icy floor, then forced myself into jeans and a sweater before I crept down the stairs.

At the top of the stairs leading to the storage rooms, I began to feel foolish. What if I did catch Nat red-handed, what could I say to him? "Excuse me, but have you just been smuggling?" After all, it was his house. He could do what he liked in it, couldn't he? Then another thought struck me—what if it wasn't Nat at all, but someone else, a big, old, ugly man who knew about the secret entrance? What if he grabbed me and I yelled and there was only Aunt Harriet to hear and she couldn't get down the stairs on her crutches?

Maybe going down there wasn't such a good idea after all. OK, I said to myself. Go back up to bed. Turn down the one exciting moment of your whole summer.

My courage and sense of adventure fought with my desire to slink back upstairs. I'll go carefully, I told myself. I'll stay out of sight. Just like in the spy movies. . . .

I crept down the steps slowly, peering into the darkness. I couldn't see anything. Then I moved forward, inch by inch, across the old basement floor. The place was a mess, full of boxes and nets and lobster pots and floats, not to mention a couple of iron bedsteads and an old sewing machine that looked as if it belonged in the Singer Museum. I stood in the shadows and listened. No more noise. Perhaps he had already gone. I went forward, making no sound. Then suddenly a figure reared up from behind some crates. That time I didn't scream. I was too scared. I opened my mouth, but no scream came out.

"What the heck do you think you're doing?" Nat Franklin asked angrily. "You nearly scared me out of my wits."

Then, as the terror left me, I saw that he looked as white and shaken as I felt.

"A person doesn't expect to look up at five in the morning and see someone standing beside him!" Nat went on. "I thought I was seeing a ghost!"

"A strange noise woke me up," I said, "and I thought I had better come down and see what it was."

"You've got guts, I'll say that for you," Nat said. "What if it had been a couple of burglars with guns?"

"What, stealing the old bed frames?" I asked and laughed.

Suddenly I noticed that he was smiling. "Are you implying there's nothing worth stealing in my house?" he asked.

"Well—it is a bit . . ." I broke off.

"Old and broken down?" he finished for me. "Yes, I guess you're right. There isn't much worth stealing here."

"By the way," he said hesitantly, "if you happen to be down in town, Meredith—your name *is* Meredith, isn't it?—don't mention to anyone that you saw me here."

"Oh?" I said, raising an eyebrow. "And why not?"

"I'd just rather my father didn't know, that's all," he said, and although it was fairly dark, I think he was blushing.

"I see," I said, enjoying this conversation.

Here I was in a position of power over Nat Franklin! "And I think I can guess why not."

"You can?" He looked alarmed.

"It's in that bag, isn't it?" I said, pointing to the big sack on the floor beside him.

"How did you know?"

"I'm not stupid. I saw you sneaking through the house twice before. I guessed. After all, you had the example of all those ancestors, didn't you?"

"I did?" He looked confused.

"So what is it?" I asked him. "Contraband? Jewels?"

"What?" He stared at me, openmouthed.

"Don't pretend you don't know what I'm talking about. I mean the smuggling."

"Smuggling?" he said, trying to stop a smile from spreading across his face. "You think I'm smuggling? I'm afraid you've been reading too many history books."

"Well, what's in the bag then?" I asked, bending down to pick it up.

"Don't put your hand in there," he said sharply.

"So you don't want me to find out, is that it?" I said as I calmly untied the knot on the bag.

"No, you idiot, you'll get pinched!" he shouted and snatched the bag from me as something snapped up at me and almost got my finger.

"Look," he said, holding the bag open. "This is what I've been smuggling."

"Oh," I said lamely. "Lobsters."

"Yes," he said, "I've been out lobster fishing. Now are you satisfied?"

I was wishing the floor would open up and swallow me. I could feel my cheeks blush fiery red. So much for the great detective act. "But why didn't you want anyone to know?" I asked. "Is it against the law or something?"

"Of course not. I have my fishing permit," he said. "It's my father I don't want to find out." He knelt down and did up the bag with string again. "You see, he runs the restaurant in town, and he likes me to bring him all the lobsters I catch. But he doesn't pay me much for them. That's why I like to sell them to the hotel over in Littlehampton. They pay really well, and I'm saving up for a car. So I've been sneaking out at night and catching my quota then. I store all my gear here." Suddenly his face broke into a big grin. "Is that why you screamed that day at the supermarket—because you thought you'd come face to face with a smuggler?"

"No," I said uncomfortably. "I thought I'd come face to face with a ghost!"

Chapter Nine

There have only been a couple of times in my life when I felt really, truly embarrassed. Once was at the age of seven when the stretched-out elastic in my tights gave out during a ballet recital and my tights slipped down to my ankles. The other time was when I was in fourth grade—I hadn't been paying attention in class, and I gave the answer to the wrong question, and everybody laughed.

But never, in my entire life, had I felt worse than I had that morning. After Nat left, I replayed the morning's events over and over. I thought I had turned into a pretty smooth sort of person, one who went around with the right crowd and had a fantastic boyfriend and knew how to flip her hair just right, and now here I was again, feeling like a second-grader.

Darn you, Nat Franklin, I thought. Why did you have to make me sound like such a fool? You didn't have to laugh so hard at what was a perfectly reasonable misunderstanding! After all, you looked scared when you saw me standing down in the cellar. And I don't even look like someone two hundred years old.

I squirmed with embarrassment every time I thought about our early-morning conversation in the basement. I'll never go down to town again, I thought. He's probably told everyone about me by now, and they're all laughing. I could just see what would happen if I ever appeared in the supermarket again. People would laugh behind my back, and someone would say, "Oh, you're the one who thought Nat was a ghost!"

Hurry up and get well quickly, Aunt Harriet, I prayed silently, so that I can go back home.

I felt terribly homesick. I suppose I thought about it so much because I was bored and because the weather was so bad. I wasn't used to rain like that. At home it rained sometimes, but when it did, it was a hard, sudden downpour, and we stayed in until it stopped. Here it never really stopped. It slowed down to a fine, wet mist, and if I ever tried to go out for a walk, the wet mist instantly turned into real rain again.

My homesickness reached its peak when I got my first letter from my family, and, on the same day—miracle of miracles—one from Peter. I opened the one from the family first. It was long and newsy and loving, full of cute anecdotes about things our cat had done and the weird flavors of ice cream they were having for dessert every night, and that alone was enough to bring tears to the eyes of someone who had to finish up dinner with goat's milk yogurt and honey! Kelly had written me a page of her own—all sweetness and love now that she had gotten her own way, which was typical Kelly. The lifeguarding was *such* fun, and there were some really *cute* boys who were lifeguards, too, but the sun had been *so* hot that she had a bad sunburn on her back, and the doctor said she had to wear a T-shirt for the rest of the summer.

Gee, Kelly, I thought, what a shame, having to hide your lovely red-and-white suit under a T-shirt, which shows you what a nasty person I really am! Actually I'm not, but Kelly, being a year older and a lot smarter, has spent her whole life getting the better of me, so you can hardly blame me for a few moments of triumph.

Steve hadn't written at all, except to add comments, in red ink, on the other two letters—things like "That's just what she's telling you. Actually it was a disaster!"—which were typically Steve.

Peter's letter was a big disappointment after the nice long one my family had sent. Of course, he had told me he wasn't very good at writing letters, but I had expected something—well, a little more personal. I had taken the letter up to my bedroom, and I read it curled up on the bed with Nat's ancestor smiling down at me.

Peter had started off with a plain old "Dear Meredith." Then he just said that he had been promoted to cook at Hamburger Haven and that it was hard, hot work cooking hamburgers all day. He told me I didn't know how lucky I was to have an ocean right at my doorstep. He did have the decency to say that the evenings were boring without me, but the rest of the gang was trying to keep him occupied. Then he told me about three new records he had bought. Finally, as a sort of P.S., he added that he was looking forward to a break on the Fourth of July weekend. Marnie's folks had rented a cabin on a lake, and he had been invited to go with them.

"Marnie has been taking good care of me, you'll be pleased to know," he said.

Hmmm—I wonder about that, I thought nervously. Peter hasn't ever been to a cabin with *me*!

"How about that?" I asked the portrait. "I bet you wouldn't have gone to a cabin with your girl's best friend!"

"I might have," the face seemed to say.

All men are the same, I thought bitterly. You can't trust any of them.

So what would or could I do about it? I could hardly rush to the phone and plead "Don't go!" Part of me kept saying that Marnie's folks were just being nice and that Marnie was just doing what I asked her to do: keeping an eye on Peter for me. But another part of me argued back—yes, but in a cabin together?

I knew I didn't have to worry: Marnie wasn't Peter's type. She was shy around boys, and she wasn't even interested in them. Still, I was worried anyway.

I decided not to think about it and to spend my time writing back to my parents instead of concentrating on Peter and Marnie. I realized how very little I had done so far this summer. All I had done was to sit and sulk and wait to hear from Peter. I had wasted nearly two whole weeks. After all, as Peter had said, I had an ocean right beside me, and there I was, not even taking advantage of it.

"Well, it's about time I do take advantage of it," I said. I peered out of the window and found to my amazement that it wasn't raining anymore.

After pondering what to do, I wandered into Aunt Harriet's study. "Aunt Harriet," I said, "is there anything you need done now? Because if you don't want anything right now, I think I'll go to the beach."

"About time you went somewhere," Aunt Harriet murmured, not looking up from her typewriter. "Have a good time. Now where was I? Ah, yes, the light in the tower . . ." and she went back to working as if I didn't even exist.

I went to my room and put on my bright yellow shorts with the matching halter top. My skin looked pale against the yellow, and I decided that if I got nothing else accomplished all summer, I, at least, had to go home with a tan. I could just imagine someone saying at school, "You spent all summer at the ocean, and you're still *that* pale?" Well, nobody was going to say that to me. Quickly I grabbed my new sketchbook and paints, a towel, sunglasses, and a Snickers bar, in case I needed a sugar fix. Then I headed outside.

The weather still wasn't great. The sun was shining at the moment, but big puffy clouds were threatening in the distance. But I wouldn't even be able to lie down on the sand if I couldn't find my way down to the beach. I walked the whole length of the garden wall before I found an archway, hidden behind brambles, which led to steps going down the cliff. The steps were cleverly cut into the rock of the cliff, so that from down below they probably couldn't even be seen. I bet they were cut by smugglers! I thought to myself, and wondered if Nat. . . . I stopped. I had forbidden myself to think about Nat again. Thoughts about him only ended up with me feeling hot and embarrassed.

At the bottom of the cliff, the steps opened out onto a perfect little sandy beach that had huge boulders on it. Next to the rocks there were pretty little tide pools. I had studied tide pools in biology, and I spent some time peering into them, identifying things I had previously only seen in textbooks. It was amazing to me that starfish really did look like stars and that sea anemones really did look like brightly colored flowers. Transparent shrimp darted from rock to rock, and a little green crab waved his pincers at me before scuttling out of sight.

If only I'd known this was at the bottom of the cliff before, I thought, I would have come down a lot sooner. But the only thing visible from the windows of the house was the ocean, and it had looked anything but friendly. That day, for the first time, the waves were small and gentle. As I walked along the edge of the water, waves rolled up to my feet shyly, then quickly rolled back down again. But the water was icy cold; so, as lovely as the ocean looked, I knew I wouldn't be going swimming that day. Unlike Kelly, I am not a super swimmer, and water has to be practically bathtub temperature before I'll dare to get wet.

But at least I can start to work on that tan, I decided. In the bright sunlight I looked even paler than I'd looked indoors. Aunt Harriet had told me that the mailman had said that we were in for a dry spell, so I decided I'd make the most of it and expose my body as much as possible. If Kelly had to spend the summer under a T-shirt, I could not lose the golden opportunity to go home with a fabulous tan!

I found a big flat rock that jutted out into the water. I climbed up, spread my towel on it, and got out my paints, a jar of water I had brought along, and my sketchbook. Last year in school we had done a bit of watercolor work, so I knew how to get started. The sun was warm on my back, and I sloshed wet paints onto wet paper in the hope of making it look something like the ocean and sky that lay before me.

After the first couple of tries, I began to get the hang of it, and my watercolored waves really did look real. I was very pleased with myself. There you are—all these years and you never knew you were a second Picasso, I said to myself. Then I decided to try to paint an island I saw in the distance to the right. From where I sat, it seemed to be floating like a shaggy green ball on top of the water.

That painting turned out to be a lot harder than the other one. My first attempt really did look like a green hairy ball and not like an island covered with trees. My second try was a bit better. I was concentrating on my painting so hard that I didn't know that someone had come up behind me in a boat to my left until that someone spoke.

"No, I guess you're not a mermaid," said the voice.

I jumped and turned, knocking over my water jar. A rowboat was rocking gently a few yards away, and in it, grinning delightedly, was Nat Franklin.

"When I saw all that hair glinting gold in the sun, I thought I'd found one at last," he said, still grinning. "What a letdown—to find it was only you!"

"I was just painting that island," I said frostily, "if that's all right with you. This seemed like the perfect spot to do it."

"Perfect," he agreed, "except for one thing— how do you plan to get back to shore?"

"I can walk very well, thank you," I said.

"Really. I didn't know anyone had the talent for walking on water these days."

I turned around and looked in horror. Where there had been sand and rocks and tide pools, the water now lapped right up to the cliff. Only the biggest rocks like mine poked their heads above it. I had no idea that water could come up so fast or so silently, but I was not going to let Nat Franklin know that I was afraid.

"I don't mind getting a bit wet," I said bravely. "I can wade back."

"OK," Nat said. "If you don't want to be rescued, that's fine. I'll stay and watch."

I collected my things and crammed them into my bag. Then I remembered that the rock I was sitting on had been a good bit taller than me and the water around it was probably now a good bit deeper than me.

"There's no way you can do it without getting all your things wet," Nat said after I had stood doing nothing for a couple of minutes. "Unless you can swim with that bag on your head. And it's not that easy with all the submerged rocks and things."

The thought of my swimming that distance among jagged rocks even without anything on my head was far from appealing! I could hardly manage that far in a swimming pool without stopping and holding on to the side. "Then I guess I need help after all," I said. "Maybe you can just row me in to where it's a bit shallower."

Nat swung the boat skillfully to the side of the rock, took my hand, and helped me down.

"I won't take you in to shore right here," he said. "There's too much risk to my boat with the rocks. I'll have to row you around the point and into our bay."

"OK. Thanks," I said, curling my toes in embarrassment. "I guess you've just saved me from a watery grave."

"Oh, I don't think you'd have gotten much more than wet," he said, pulling strongly on the oars to turn the boat around. We seemed to shoot across the water. "But for future reference, you'd better check the tides before you go climbing on the rocks again."

"I didn't realize," I said sheepishly. "I've never seen an ocean before, and lakes don't really have tides!"

"Never seen an ocean?" he repeated with shock. "I didn't think there were such underprivileged people in the world anymore."

"Underprivileged!" I said angrily. "Why, if you lived in the Midwest like me you would know thousands of people who've never seen an ocean. Just think how much it costs to travel this far."

"Hmmm—I guess you're right," he said thoughtfully. "I've never been more than a hundred miles away from the ocean in my entire life. I suppose I take it for granted. I don't think I could live without it."

"I bet you've never seen a prairie—stretching flat as far as the eye can see," I said. "Or a tornado."

He smiled. "You're right, I haven't. But don't tell me you can't live without tornadoes."

"I'll let you in on a secret," I said. "I've never actually seen one either. But I did see the damage one had done once, and I can happily live without them."

For a while we rowed in silence. There was no sound except for the rhythmic creaking of the oars and the slapping of water against the hull. The sun was warm on my back. I thought how nice it would be to close my eyes and relax. What a perfect scene to write home to Marnie about: "And there I was, being rowed along this fabulous shoreline by an even more fabulous boy . . ." Then I came back to reality and remembered that that fabulous boy thought I was the world's biggest idiot. He had stood there grinning while I thought he was a ghost, then a smuggler. He had grinned again when I was hopelessly cut off by the tide. Why did things have to work that way? Whenever I wanted to make a good impression on someone, I always made the worst impression! I stopped in mid-thought, rather surprised at what I was thinking. I hadn't realized until then that I had wanted to make a good impression on Nat, that I had wanted him to notice me. I had thought that being Peter's girl was enough and that I'd never look at anyone else.

But if Peter's going off to a cabin with a strange girl, who luckily only happened to be Marnie, I decided that it was OK for me to enjoy myself a little, too.

I opened my eyes. Nat was looking straight at me. Again I was struck by those tiger eyes. He shook his head and smiled at the same time. "Never seen an ocean," he muttered and went on rowing.

Well, you can abandon any thoughts about Nat Franklin, I told myself severely. He thinks you're a weirdo as well as a fool.

Suddenly something hurtled from the sky and splashed into the water a few feet from us. I jumped, of course. I had no idea what it might be, and I wondered if anybody could be shooting at us, but Nat didn't seem worried. Then a white-feathered head broke through the water, followed by the large white body of a bird.

"Oh," I said with relief in my voice. "It's only a gull."

"Gannet," Nat said.

"Pardon me?"

"It's not a gull, it's a gannet. They fly high above the water, then they dive for fish. He missed that time. Most of the time they don't miss.

"Of course, the cormorants are the best at catching fish under water. They swim so fast that they can chase a fish and catch it. Which is pretty remarkable when you see how fast fish swim."

I remembered what my aunt had said—that he was interested in wildlife. Well, it was certainly true. Nat's face became very animated when he talked about seabirds.

We had rounded the point and were coming toward a jetty down below a dark brown wooden house. The house was as neat and simple as a child's first drawing of his family's home; it had two windows upstairs and two downstairs, a big front door, and a steep triangular roof with a chimney poking out of it. I compared it with Stormhaven and could understand that after living in that big, old place, the Franklins might want to live somewhere very simple.

Nat looked toward his house and then back at me. "Drat," he said. "I was going to offer you a ride up the hill, but my dad's already taken the truck, and I don't think you'd fit on my ten-speed."

"That's OK," I said. "The walk will be good for me." But mentally I cursed his father for taking that truck, just when Nat seemed to be starting to treat me as a normal human being and not as a freak.

Skillfully he brought the boat alongside the jetty, stood up, and grabbed one of the posts, sliding the rope that was attached to the boat around it. He swung himself up, then helped me out of the rowboat and onto the jetty.

"Thank you very much for rescuing me," I

said formally as we headed up toward his house. "I hope I didn't take you out of your way."

"Oh, I wasn't going anywhere special," he said, smiling. "Sometimes I just like to row around and watch things. There's so much to see—seals and birds—once I even saw a whale."

"You did?" I asked in amazement. I had a horrible vision of a huge body rearing up beside the tiny boat.

"It was way out to sea, but I saw it blow. Then it waggled its tail a couple of times," Nat said.

"You know, being with you is like having a *National Geographic* TV special with me," I said, "or coming face to face with Jacques Cousteau!"

"Didn't you know they call me the Jacques Cousteau of the northern shore?" Nat asked, grinning. Then he looked thoughtful for a moment. "I don't suppose you've ever tasted fresh clams, have you?" he asked. "Not having seen an ocean before or anything."

"I've never tasted any clams, fresh or otherwise," I admitted.

"That's terrible. To have lived so long in ignorance. Look, there's going to be a clambake on Saturday night. You want to come?"

"Sure," I said. "I'd love to."

"Great," he said. "I'll come by and pick you up around eight." He walked to his front door and turned the knob, but just as he was about to go in, he turned around. "Oh, and wear old clothes," Nat yelled, grinning. Then with a wave of his big hand, he turned back again and went into his house.

I don't remember climbing up the hill to get home. I think I floated.

Chapter Ten

I thought I knew about clambakes. I could remember seeing one in an old musical on TV. People lit big fires on the beach and cooked clams on them and danced around singing that they were all having a "real good time." And it didn't look like they were wearing their old clothes, either! The women had bonnets and long skirts and lots of petticoats.

So when it came time to decide what to wear on what might possibly be described as a date with Nat Franklin, I didn't really want it to be old clothes. Besides, I didn't have any old clothes with me, unless designer jeans, six months old, could be counted as old.

"I'm so excited," I told Aunt Harriet. I was beginning to like her a little more these days, though I still thought of her as kind of weird.

"I'm sure you'll have a lovely time, Meredith, but you should dress more sensibly. "It's going to get pretty cold down there on the beach," Aunt Harriet warned me from her seat on my bed, frowning as I tried on a silky pink top and matching pink jeans.

"But what about all the driftwood fires and dancing and stuff?"

"It'll still be pretty cold, my dear."

"OK," I said and changed from the pink outfit into blue jeans and a white sweat shirt with a rainbow across the front of it.

"Can I do anything for you before I leave, Aunt Harriet?"

"No, Meredith. Just run along and have a good time."

When Nat arrived, he eyed me suspiciously. "Are those what you call old clothes?" he asked. "You're going to get them awful dirty."

"They're all washable," I said, rather annoyed that he had not told me how nice I looked.

"And what's that you've got on your feet?" He sounded as if I had something awful—like warts all over my toes.

I looked down in surprise. "They're only ordinary sandals."

"Don't you have any boots?"

"Boots!" I was really getting annoyed now. "Nope. No boots."

"Can't you borrow a pair from your aunt?" I had seen Aunt Harriet's boots. They were the sort of boots people wear on farms—big, clompy, shapeless black rubber boots. There was no way I was going to wear them. "Er— we're not the same size," I said hastily. "My feet are a lot bigger. Besides, I don't feel the cold. I'm used to cold winters where I come from, remember?"

"I'll see if I can borrow a pair of boots for you when we get there," Nat said firmly. "Grab your parka and let's get going."

When I took down a blue satin wind jacket from its hook in the hall, Nat almost looked despairing.

"Don't tell me you don't have a parka," he said, then sighed.

"Well, I came expecting summer on the beach. I didn't think I'd have to bring my ski clothes," I said. "This is the warmest thing I have."

"Well, I suppose it will have to do, then," Nat said.

Thank heavens he didn't suggest I borrow Aunt Harriet's coat. The only coat of hers I had seen was a moldy green one, and I would rather have frozen into a block of ice than have worn that.

But when I climbed into the truck next to Nat and we set off down the hill, I forgot all about clothes, and about everything else, for that matter. We drove through town and out the other side, then we turned off onto a trail and bumped through pine woods. Suddenly the pine woods ended, and before us was a little sheltered bay. The sun had just set, and the whole scene still glowed with a warm, pink light. The tide was way out, and there was a huge stretch of wet sand, striped with silver streaks of water. Beyond it the ocean seemed to be made of pure silver edged with pink waves. It was a magical scene.

On the beach there was already quite a crowd of people, young and old and in-between. Just like in the old movie, there was a driftwood fire already going strong—red sparks leaped up and twigs crackled every few seconds.

As Nat and I jumped down from the truck, some kids noticed us and called out.

"Here's Nat now!" one voice yelled out.

"Better late than never!" yelled another voice.

Someone else called, "What took you so long? We've been waiting for you to get started."

"Couldn't you start without me to show you how?" Nat asked, teasing them back.

"We wanted to make sure you didn't get out of your share of the work, that's all," called the first voice.

"I always do my share—besides, I had to go and pick somebody up."

I felt my cheeks turning as pink as the evening sky as the group of faces suddenly noticed me for the first time.

"I thought it was Sandi," someone said in a low voice.

"No, it's not Sandi," Nat said hastily. "This is Meredith, and she's staying with her aunt up at Stormhaven."

All the kids smiled at me politely, and one or two of them said, "Hi, Meredith." A red-haired boy grinned at me and said, "I bet you're having fun being stuck in that cold, drafty, termite-ridden old place."

"Stormhaven is not termite ridden," Nat said fiercely. "Just because your family has no history, or else it's so shameful you don't want to talk about it—"

"Yeah, didn't you know," someone else jumped in, "that Robbie's grandfather was a pirate who jumped ship?"

Everyone laughed.

I was forgotten again, a stranger in a group

of old friends. Being alone gave me a moment to wonder who Sandi was and to feel a stab of jealousy I should never have felt.

"Come on, you guys," one of the girls pleaded. "It's going to be dark soon, and we won't be able to see what we're doing."

"I'll just feel my way then," one of the boys said, and the girl squealed as he grabbed her.

"No, seriously, Sammy," the girl said insistently, "let's get going, you guys."

"Yeah, come on. The stuff's over here."

The group broke up. Robbie, the redhead, came over to Nat and me. "Here, choose your weapons," he said as he handed us a spade and a bucket.

"What are these for?" I asked stupidly.

Nat looked surprised. "It's a small matter of having to dig for some clams before we can eat them," he said. "Here, take the bucket and come with me. I'll show you what to do."

He took the spade and turned toward the ocean, stomping in his big boots over the wet sand. His footprints made holes that turned silver as they filled with water. I followed bravely. I was rapidly beginning to understand why old clothes were necessary.

At first the sand was hard and firm, but as we got farther out, I felt one of my nice white sandals sink into the cold, gooey mud. I wrenched it out, and it came up with a horrible sucking sound.

"How do we find the clams?" I asked, trying hard to keep up with Nat and his huge strides.

"Just look for their holes," he said. "See—here's one." He pointed with the spade to a tiny crater in the wet ooze. Then he dug his spade in and lifted out a big chunk of sand.

"There, quick," he said. "Grab it while you can see it, before the hole fills with water."

I knelt down and plunged my hand into the cold, wet hole. Water seeped up past my elbow. My fingers closed on ooze, but not on any clam. I didn't know anything about clams, and I was scared it might shut my finger in its shell—like the giant clams in movies. Anyway, I came up empty-handed.

"You weren't quick enough," Nat said. "That one got away. They burrow downward, you know. You've got to grab it as soon as I turn over the sand."

I don't want to go into too much detail about the next hour. I think unpleasant scenes are best glossed over, and anyway, nobody else would be interested in hearing about the sheer torture of standing up to my ankles in freezing water, kneeling down in freezing water, and plunging my arm into freezing water just to bring up one tiny clam. Of course, after I found out that they weren't going to snap shut on my fingers, I felt a bit better about picking them up, but they were just plain hard to find in the wet mud.

In the end not only my teeth but my whole body was chattering. My jeans were so plastered with mud that I cracked as I moved. But I kept right on. The honor of the Midwest was at stake. I didn't want Nat to think that girls from Chicago were cowards or quitters. To be honest, I didn't care too much about what he thought of other Chicago girls, but I wanted him to think I was doing OK. He seemed quite happy, standing there in his huge parka, big sea boots, and woolly cap, digging up huge chunks of wet sand.

"Do you think we've got enough yet?" I asked, when I felt I couldn't stand it any longer.

He looked at the bucket, at me, and at the other diggers. Then he smiled—a smile that would have made any girl instantly warm again.

"Yeah, I guess we've got enough. I told you you'd freeze in that outfit, didn't I? Come on, let's get you back to the fire."

We walked back across the sand to where dark shapes were moving around the fire.

From a distance they seemed like a primitive tribe, carrying out a sacrifice or a war dance.

"Is that all you got?" someone jeered as Nat handed over our pail.

"Yes, well, Meredith is new to this, don't forget," Nat answered.

"Don't give me that excuse," one of the boys said, teasing us. "You two were busy doing other things—"

"Come on, Meredith," Nat said, taking my arm and hastily steering me away, "let's go and get you warm. They should have some hot coffee going by now."

Over by the fire some adults and one or two little kids were busy with plates and bread. Someone was stirring a mysterious pot that steamed like a witch's caldron.

"What have we got to warm up a frozen person?" Nat asked for me. "Any coffee?"

"Coffee's not ready yet," the woman at the fire said cheerfully. "What about a mug of chowder? I made it this morning, and I thought it might come in handy."

"Here," Nat said, handing me the mug. His fingers brushed against mine.

"Hey, your hands are freezing," he said, putting down the mug on a picnic table.

"I'm freezing all over," I admitted.

"You'd better have this." He unzipped his parka.

"No, I couldn't take your parka," I said.

"Don't be silly. Then you'd be cold."

"I'm fine," he said as he gently put his jacket around me. "I've got my sweater underneath, and besides, I'm a very warm-blooded person."

Suddenly I was very conscious of his arms slowly pulling the parka around me, pulling me toward him until our lips were a fraction of an inch apart.

"Naughty, naughty," came a voice from behind us, and there was Robbie, grinning again.

"You'd better behave yourself, or I'll have to tell Sandi!" he taunted.

"And you'd better get lost, or I'll bury you in that sand," Nat answered, but he didn't try again to kiss me.

Darn this Sandi, whoever she is, I thought as we sat there sipping hot chowder. Then I had a sudden unsettling thought: was someone, right then, saying to Peter, "I'll have to tell Meredith"?

I sighed out loud. Nat turned and looked at me.

"What's wrong?" he asked gently.

"I was just wondering why life has to be so complicated," I said.

"Yes, it is, isn't it?" he agreed. He moved closer to me and put his arm around me. "Still cold?" he asked.

I smiled up at him. "No, I'm just fine now. You sure you don't want your parka back?"

He shook his head. "I told you I was warm-blooded," he said and kept his arm around my shoulder.

We were still sitting like that when Aileen came by. "Oh, it's you, Meredith," she said, looking surprised. "My brother told me that Nat had this strange girl with him, so I just had to come over and see who it was."

"Your brother?" I asked. Light was beginning to dawn on me. "Oh, Robbie—is he your brother?"

"You don't think we'd allow two families of redheads in one town, do you?" Nat asked.

Aileen made a face at him. "Well, you just watch out for him, Meredith," she said, giving me a knowing look.

"Oh, Meredith knows I'm completely trustworthy, don't you?" he asked, giving my shoulder a little squeeze.

"Then she's dumb," Aileen said. "If she trusts you."

"So now I'm dumb as well as strange," I said and laughed. "I don't think you have a very high opinion of me."

"Oh, you know what I mean," Aileen said. "I didn't mean really strange or really dumb—I just meant—"

"Aileen, get lost, will you?" Nat interrupted.

"I can tell when I'm not wanted," Aileen said, pretending to be offended. She turned to leave, but as she went she leaned down to me and whispered, "We have friendly ghosts around here, don't we?"

It was a wonderful evening. We ate clams that had been steamed under seaweed, and we had crusty bread with them. When we were too full to eat any more, someone brought out a guitar, and everybody sang.

It was so different from evenings at home. If anyone had suggested to my friends there that we wear dirty old clothes and sing songs around a fire, we would have laughed and joked about leaving that sort of thing to the Boy Scouts.

And yet, there I was, having a great time, joining in the chorus as loudly as anyone. Had I ever had a great time like this at home? When we had parties where we slow danced or listened to loud rock, did I really feel as alive and happy as I did then?

"I hope we simple folks weren't too boring for a slick city girl like you," Nat said as we walked back to the truck later on.

"I think I just had one of the best evenings of my life," I answered. And I meant it.

Chapter Eleven

Nat and I drove home in silence. The moon had risen, and it hung like a big silver bubble suspended over the ocean. It was an enchanted night, but inside the truck there was tension between us. I was very aware of Nat's presence beside me. We were sitting just far enough apart so that we weren't touching, but a sort of electric current passed through the space between us. I knew that Nat was as attracted to me as I was to him, but before anything could happen between us, there was an unspoken question that had to be answered—a final barrier that had to be knocked down. At last I could stand it no longer and had to ask.

"Who's Sandi?"

"Sandi?" he asked, then he paused. I was

sure he was about to say something light like, "Oh she's just a girl I know," but he didn't. He took a deep breath and said, "She's my girlfriend. She's from Boston. Her folks rent a house here for the summer, and she's arriving next week."

"Oh," I said. "So it's pretty serious, huh?"

"Yes," he said. "Pretty serious, I guess. She's a special sort of girl—you'll see when you meet her."

"Oh," I said again. I must have sounded like an idiot.

"What about you?" he asked after a while. "What did you mean when you said that life was complicated, back there on the beach?"

"I was thinking about my boyfriend at home," I said hesitantly.

"And you promised to remain faithful and true all summer?" Nat asked. "Only now you're so far away and you're wondering?"

"Sort of," I said. "I thought I knew how I felt about him. I thought I'd never feel that way about anyone else. Only—only now I'm not so sure. He's spending the weekend at a cabin with my best friend."

"The dirty rat," Nat said and grinned.

I couldn't help but smile. "Well, it isn't so bad as it sounds—I hope," I added quickly. "It was her family who invited him."

"That's what they always say," Nat said.

I looked across at him and smiled. His hand came across the seat of the truck to touch mine.

"Back there on the beach I wanted to kiss you," he said.

"I know."

"Would you have minded?"

"I suppose I should have, but I knew I wouldn't have minded at all."

Nat brought the truck to a halt on the side of the road. "What about now?" he asked, and without waiting for an answer, he drew me gently toward him, and his lips were brushing mine—questioningly at first, then hungrily. I had meant to protest, I think, but even if I had meant to—I forgot.

When we finally drew apart, guilt overcame me. "Nat, what about Sandi?"

"What about Horace or what's-his-name at the cabin?"

"It's Peter, and he's a thousand miles away."

"And Sandi doesn't get here for another week," he said. Then he kissed me again.

"I think I'd better go, Nat," I pleaded a few moments later. I was trying to fight the confusion that was spinning around in my head.

"Maybe you're right," he said, those tiger eyes of his glowing at me in the dark. "Before we both get too involved—" He started up the engine again, and soon we were roaring up the hill.

I said good night, as soon as we pulled up beside the steps leading up to the house, then climbed down from the cab before he could kiss me again.

"Thank you for a wonderful evening," I called out to him.

He grinned at me. "I hope the mud washes out of those clothes," he called back. "And that you don't die of double pneumonia!"

"Don't worry, I won't." I turned to walk toward the steps.

"Meredith," he called after me. I looked back.

"Can I see you again? Soon, I mean?"

I opened my mouth to say that we ought to be fair to Sandi and Peter and that we shouldn't see each other tomorrow or ever, but instead I heard myself saying, "If you want to."

After I had watched the truck drive away down the hill and had gone up to the house, I became fully aware of my guilt and confusion. "Meredith Markham, what have you done now?" I asked myself. I hadn't meant to get involved with Nat, really I hadn't. He was great looking, he was fun but—I had meant to keep him just as a friend I met on a summer vacation. Nothing more than that. I had thought I could never feel this way with any-one but Peter. But now I knew it was already too late. I knew how I felt about Nat. He was not just someone I met one summer. And I knew that when Sandi finally arrived, my heart would break.

The next week I was full of both hope and despair. Hope that when Sandi arrived Nat would find that he liked me better than her and despair because he probably wouldn't.

It seemed as if two different voices were fighting inside me. There was the voice that kept reminding me about Peter and about Sandi and how I had to be fair to everybody. Then there was the other voice that whispered about all being fair in love and war and that if I took Nat away from Sandi that was just too bad.

After all, I decided, or rather the aggressive voice in me decided, I am not bad looking. I dress nicely. I'm intelligent. I should be a match for any old Sandi. It's not my fault that she didn't get here until a week too late!

I'm afraid that this voice was winning out over the other voice. The good little girl part of me thought that maybe I should try to avoid Nat. But the other part of me just wouldn't go along with that.

When Nat didn't call for a couple of days, I began to feel very down. "You see," I said to myself. "All that worrying about what was right and what was wrong for nothing. He's not even going to see you again before Sandi arrives."

Even Aunt Harriet, busy as she was with rescuing Camilla from the terrible music master and his snake, noticed I was acting weirdly.

"Is something happening out there?" she asked me as I brought in her tea and just happened to let my gaze stray out of the window.

"No, why?" I asked.

"Because you seem to be spending a large percentage of your time staring out windows. You're not expecting a visitor, are you?"

"No, of course not," I said, angry at myself for blushing.

"Oh, well, I just wondered," Aunt Harriet said smoothly, going back to her work and smiling a little. Then she looked up again. "You know, I really don't need you this afternoon if you want to take a little stroll downtown. You never know whom you might meet, do you?"

"No, thank you, Aunt Harriet," I replied firmly. "I'm quite happy up here with you."

"Ah—you don't want it to seem that you're running after him," she said.

"I don't know what you mean," I said, feeling my cheeks turning an even brighter shade of crimson.

She laughed. "Strange though it may seem, I was young once, too," she said. "And Nat Franklin is a very attractive-looking boy. I wouldn't mind him myself if I were forty years younger."

"Nat already has a girlfriend," I said.

"So I hear," Aunt Harriet said, calmly correcting her typing. "This town is pretty small, you know. Which means I am also aware of the fact that she's not here right now. And he's not engaged to her or anything. Please pick up some kelp tablets for me when you pass the natural foods store."

Now that I had an errand to run for her, I had to go down to town. Pretty crafty of Aunt Harriet. Well, I didn't have to speak to anyone while I was there or go looking for ex-ghosts or smugglers.

I tried to walk down Main Street purposefully, as if I had only come to buy kelp tablets. The first person I bumped into was Aileen.

"Well, hi, stranger," she said. "You look like you're in a hurry."

"I've got some things to buy for my aunt."

"Emergency supplies of soybeans?" she asked, laughing.

"Kelp tablets, actually."

Aileen made a face. "Yuck. The junk that woman eats. Does that mean you don't have time for a hamburger with me at the motel?"

I weakened. "Nothing in the world could make me miss the chance for a hamburger," I said.

"Not even Nat Franklin?" she asked, smiling slyly as we headed toward the motel. "You seemed to be getting on *very* well with him the other night. You made a lovely couple sitting together in the moonlight."

I sighed and then was silent, not knowing what to say.

"That's some achievement," she went on, "making Nat Franklin look at another woman. That's unheard of. It must be your midwestern charm."

"Well, Sandi gets here soon, so I guess he's already forgotten I exist," I said.

She looked at me with interest. "Now what makes you think that?" she asked.

"I haven't seen him since the night of the clambake."

"There's such a thing as having to work for his dad," she said.

"I forgot about that," I said, remembering that his dad ran a restaurant.

She smiled. "Well, Miss Meredith, it might

interest you to know that I have a message for you."

"You do? From whom?"

"Who do you think?"

I blushed for the third time that day.

"He stopped me this morning and asked me if I was driving up your way today. Then he said, 'Tell her I've been busy, but can she keep tomorrow free for me.' "

"He did?" I asked, grinning stupidly.

"He did."

"Did he say what time?"

She shook her head. "I'm not his social secretary, you know. I expect it will be when he can get off work."

Nat appeared the next day at Stormhaven right in the middle of breakfast—luckily, after Aunt Harriet had finished eating and had gone to her study to type. He came into the kitchen without knocking, almost as silently as his ancestor the ghost.

"Don't you ever think of knocking?" I asked, frowning at him. "I might have been sitting here in my pajamas."

He gave a meaningful grin. "I'm always hopeful," he said. "But I came with an important message."

"Let me guess—the British are coming!"

"It's amazing how you outsiders think that that was the only exciting thing that ever happened in New England," he said, trying to look withering. "Actually I came to tell you something much more exciting. I came to tell you that I managed to persuade my father to give me the sailboat for the day—since I'm sure you've never been out in a real boat before."

"It's amazing how you New Englanders think that you are the only people with water!" I said, imitating his voice perfectly. "Just because we don't have an ocean doesn't mean that I have never seen a boat before, you know. We do have a little lake called Michigan in my part of the world, and you are talking to an expert sailor!"

"Oh," he said, his face falling like a little boy's. "Does that mean you don't want to come? You could take over the helm—"

"Oh, Nat," I said, "to tell you the truth, I've only been out in a sailboat once in my life, and I think I was about seven years old at the time. I know nothing about sailing, and I'd love to come. I just felt I had to defend the honor of the Great Lakes."

"Crazy female," he said. "Well, if you're coming, don't just sit there doing nothing;

110

go and get ready. We don't want to waste half the day."

I jumped up. "I won't be a minute," I said.

"Oh, Meredith," he called after me, "don't forget to wear something warm!"

I made a face at him as I left. Actually, he didn't have to remind me. I wasn't going to freeze a second time. I put on a white turtleneck under my big blue angora sweater, and I put leg warmers on over my jeans.

"OK, weather, do your worst, I'm ready for you," I said, running a quick brush through my hair and fixing it back with purple barrettes.

When I ran in to say goodbye to Aunt Harriet, I felt a twinge of guilt about leaving her all day. "You're sure you'll be all right?" I asked. "I did rinse some vegetables for your lunch."

"Of course I'll be all right," she said. It was hard to tell from her face if she was annoyed or not.

"It's just that I might not get another chance to go sailing—" I said hesitantly.

"Meredith, I said I shall be quite all right," she snapped. "Just go already."

"Well, if you're sure—"

"Meredith!" she said. "Don't keep the young man waiting any longer. Do you think I'd stand in the way of young love?" Then she gave me a ghost of a smile.

"You know, my Aunt Harriet's not bad after all," I said to Nat as we walked down the hill toward a field.

"I always thought she was an interesting old bird," he said. "It's obvious she's the person in your family who has the brains!"

"Why do you say that?"

"Well, she chose to live here, didn't she? That shows intelligence."

"You'd better watch it, or you might find yourself pushed over the cliff," I said.

"So you think you're strong enough to take me on?" he asked, teasing me, challenging me.

"Sure," I said. "Haven't I told you that I'm the wrist-wrestling champion of the state of Illinois?"

I made a grab at him, but he was too quick for me. His strong hands grasped my wrists. I struggled in vain, until he had my arms pinned at my sides.

"Do you surrender?" he asked, his eyes looking down into mine, those tiger lights flashing dangerously.

"Totally," I whispered, my heart beating so loudly that the whole world must have heard it. He gave a little laugh as his lips pressed against mine.

I don't know how long we stood there before I remembered that we were standing in full view of the road.

"Nat," I said, drawing away from him, "anyone might see."

"Let them. It's a free country," he said, his lips seeking mine again.

My conscience was fighting its own battle with my longing for him. "But, Nat," I forced myself to whisper, "what about Sandi—"

He relaxed his hold on me. "I suppose you're right," he said. "We can't let this sort of thing become a habit, can we? Come on, let's run."

He took my hand, and together we ran down the hill. The way the wind met my face made me feel as if I were flying.

"By the way," Nat called as we ran, "remind me to bring back a lobster for your Aunt Harriet. That will make her happy."

"She'll only eat it if it's organically grown, low in cholesterol, and contains no additives," I said gloomily.

Nat laughed. "Boy, you sound as if you're having a great summer!" he said.

"Well, I am now," I said, but I think I said it too quietly for him to hear.

We walked down the hill and cut across the

field toward Nat's house. Behind the house was the bay, its surface sparkling with diamonds of light. A slim white jetty stretched out into the calm waters of the small bay. At the end of the jetty, a sailboat bobbed calmly next to the rowboat Nat had rescued me with.

"There she is," Nat said with pride in his voice. "There's *Stormy Petrel*. We keep her tied up in town at the marina usually, but I just sailed her up here."

The boat was beautiful—long and white and sleek with bright blue sails. It looked as if it could go very fast, and I was glad I had told Nat the truth about my limited ability as a sailor. I certainly wouldn't have wanted to handle a thing like that in the sea!

"Nat, she's beautiful!" I took a deep breath. "But isn't she a bit big for one person to sail?"

I guess he must have heard the nervousness in my voice because he smiled and put an arm around me. "There are two of us, remember?" he said.

"Yes, but only one of us who knows what he's doing."

"Well, the one who knows what he's doing will yell at the other one, and we'll get along just fine."

114

I think I still must have looked worried because he smiled up at me as he helped me aboard. "Don't worry," he said. "She's a very easy ship to sail. I've handled her alone lots of times."

I saw right away that this was true. Nat gave me things to do, but he didn't really need my help. Soon the blue jib sail was up and ready, the mainsail was waiting to be hauled up, and we slipped away from the dock as if by magic. There was a good, stiff breeze, and *Stormy Petrel* seemed like an impatient horse at the starting gate. As soon as we were clear of the dock, Nat yelled to me to run up the mainsail.

I'm glad I didn't try to follow his order literally. Not being totally ignorant, I realized that was sailor talk for pulling the mainsail up with a rope or line, which was exactly what I did. The great sheet of blue flew upward, flapping madly in the wind until the boat turned a little. Suddenly the sail billowed out stiff with the wind, and we shot forward. Wind swept my hair back and made my cheeks sting. Blue water rushed past us, and white spray splashed up each time we met a wave. There was a fantastic sensation of speed and lightness, of freedom, almost of flying.

Again I felt as I had at the clambake, only this time the feeling was much stronger. I felt as if I had never really been alive until then and that every part of me was tingling with being alive now. I felt as if I were part of the ship and the ocean.

"How do you like it?" Nat yelled. "Feel seasick yet?"

"It's—it's just fantastic!" I yelled back. "And I feel fine!"

I looked across at Nat, and I saw that his eyes were shining, too. His strong hand was resting easily on the tiller, and he held the sail line steadily in his other hand as if it were no effort at all to make this sleek, powerful ship obey him. Sitting there at the tiller Nat looked more like the portrait than ever. I could imagine him at the helm of a pirate ship, the same glint in his eye as he outran the navy ships that were following him.

He must have sensed me watching him because he looked up at me and smiled.

"Want to try?" he asked.

"Try what?"

"Taking the tiller, of course."

"Me? Steer the boat?"

"Sure. It's not hard. Come on, give me your hand and sit down here. I'll show you how."

I edged down the deck very cautiously. I

say cautiously because the deck was at an alarming angle by this time, one side was almost totally out of the water and the other almost submerged. It was also slippery. But Nat reached out and grabbed my hand and brought me safely beside him.

"Here," he said. "Take this. Now, you see that little flag up there at the top of the mast? That shows you where the wind is coming from. You don't want to take her straight into the wind, or we won't go anywhere. So keep her on a course toward that island over there. Oh, and keep a firm grip on that line. We don't want to let out any more sail."

"Nat—really," I pleaded.

"You'll do just fine," he said. "It's no fun just sitting in a sailboat doing nothing. Besides, you have the honor of the Midwest to uphold— remember?"

I felt the tug of the tiller in one hand and the line jerking in the other. I wondered if Nat would let me drown if we capsized. I must have been gripping the tiller too hard because that little flag lined up with the sail, and we slowed down. I forced the tiller over to the right and felt the speed pick up again.

At first I was really scared, but then I started concentrating on what I was doing. And I realized that I was doing it well. Soon I wasn't scared at all. In fact, I was thrilled and excited. It was a wonderful feeling of power, having control over something as large and strong as that boat and something as wild and fierce as the Atlantic Ocean.

Nat moved back over to sit next to me.

"Do you want the tiller back?" I asked.

He shook his head. "No, keep going. You're doing just fine. In fact, you have a good feel for sailing. When Sandi tries to take control of the boat, we wander all over the ocean, and—"

He stopped short, and we both looked out over the water.

"Here, you'd better let me take over now," he said, after we had sat in silence, listening to the swish of the waves and the flap and creak of the sail. "I want to sail between those two islands, and it's a bit tricky."

His hand brushed mine as he took the tiller from me, and again I was powerfully aware of the effect any contact with him had on me. Why should I feel as if I had been hit by an electric shock each time he touched me? Even Peter had never done that to me.

We glided between two rocky islands, and Nat swung the boat into a small, sandy bay.

"Help me bring in the sails, OK?" he said. "We're going to anchor here."

I followed the commands he yelled at me in quick succession, and soon *Stormy Petrel* was bobbing happily in the sheltered bay.

"Are you hungry?" he asked.

"Starving," I admitted. "It was dumb of me not to bring some food from Aunt Harriet's. It actually did cross my mind, but I thought you wouldn't be interested in a bean curd and alfalfa sprout sandwich."

"No way," he said, wrinkling his nose. "I have something much better than that junk."

He reached down into the cabin and brought up a foil-wrapped packet. "Have one of these," he said. It was a crabmeat sandwich, about two inches thick, made on crusty French bread, and it was incredibly delicious!

"Did you make this?" I asked, "or did your mother?"

"I'll let you in on a secret," he said with his mouth half-full. "I stole them from the restaurant. Our cook had just made a whole big pile, so I just helped myself."

"Nat, you're terrible," I said, laughing.

"Well, it's too late to give it back," he said. "You've just been disposing of stolen property, so you're just as guilty as I am." He brought out another bag from the cabin. "Hmmm, I guess you don't want any stolen fruit then," he said, peering into the bag. There was a self-satisfied grin on his face. "There are peaches and grapes and—"

"I'm ready to start on a life of crime," I said. "Just hand over some grapes."

Then we lay back, eating grapes and spitting the pits into the water. This started a pit-spitting contest, which Nat won. Then he spread out a towel on top of the cabin, and we lay in the sun and just watched the waves and the sky and the birds. Nat pointed them all out to me, and I began to recognize an oyster catcher from a herring gull, which showed I was making progress.

Then I realized something. "You know what? I'm much too hot," I said, peeling off my leg warmers and sweater and rolling up my pant legs.

There was a triumphant grin on Nat's face. "Some people are never satisfied," he said.

Chapter Twelve

Everything was just perfect that day. It was perfect to lie there in the sun with half-closed eyes, feeling the warmth on my face and listening to the slap of water as it rocked us gently, the cry of the seabirds, and the soft murmur of wind in the pine trees. Best of all was having Nat that close beside me. Even though we didn't actually touch each other, I was very conscious that he was there and that our fingertips were almost touching.

Once I opened my eyes and saw that he was looking at me. For a long time our eyes held each other's. I smiled, and he moved toward me. Then I guess he must have felt guilty and remembered Sandi, because he straightened up, looked at his watch, and said, "Well, we ought to be heading back. The wind picks up by late afternoon."

Without saying another word, we both got busy. Nat hauled in the anchor, and we pulled up the sails and moved slowly out of our little bay. I looked back longingly. I don't suppose I'll ever have the chance to come here again with Nat, I thought. Sandi will show up, and then he won't have any time for me.

As we rounded the point between the two islands, we caught the full force of the wind. It hit me so strongly in the face that I found myself gulping for breath.

"Oh, no," Nat said angrily.

"What? Is there anything wrong?" I asked. I thought for a moment that I had done something to annoy him.

"It's this wind," he said. "They mentioned on the radio that a storm was coming in tonight, but I thought we'd be safely back before it came."

He screwed up his eyes and looked out over the ocean. I looked, too. Where we'd seen a rich blue sea before, merging with the paler blue of the sky, we now saw a dark, rough ocean and a gray sky. The clouds that had been fluffy and light had become thick and menacing, and they came racing toward us.

"Stay right next to that jib line and be

ready to come about when I tell you," Nat called. "We're going to have to change course a lot more. The wind between these islands gusts like you can't believe."

As I sat there at the ready with that line in my hands, I felt a thrill, not of fear but of excitement. We sailed clear of the island, and suddenly we were in the open sea. Waves rushed at us, but we cut through them with seeming ease. *Stormy Petrel* had moved fast before, but now she positively flew. Spray broke over the bow and drenched us. The feeling of speed was incredible. The ropes and sails whined and groaned in protest.

"Ready to come about," Nat yelled, and my cold, wet fingers fought to release the line and haul the sail across to the other side. The boom swung over, and we were racing in a new direction.

The mountains of clouds gathered together and turned into a solid ceiling of darkness. The wind howled at us, the waves lifed *Stormy Petrel* like a child's toy boat, and threw it forward. I began to feel scared. When Nat shouted something at me that I didn't understand and he had to shout it again, I realized that he was scared, too.

Earlier, I had tossed my warm clothes down in the cabin, and I was drenched with icy water, but I couldn't leave my post to go and get them. Even if I could have left, I'd never have made it down that crazy sloping deck. So I sat and shivered, from cold and from fear, and tried hard not to let Nat see how frozen and terrified I was.

So on it went. Nat yelled out what to do, I did it, and *Stormy Petrel* raced to beat the storm back to port. Then suddenly I realized that we weren't moving quite as quickly as before, and that the waves weren't quite as big. I looked up at the cliffs looming ahead of us, and there was Stormhaven—big and dark and spooky looking, perched on top of the cliff. I never thought I would be pleased to see that house, but I was!

"Here, help me take the sails down," Nat called. My fingers were trembling so badly that I could hardly make them obey me, but at last the mainsail was down, and we were gliding in the bay, going toward Nat's jetty. Nat seemed quite unaffected by the whole adventure, and I wondered if, in fact, those were normal sailing conditions that he sailed through all the time. He certainly looked pretty relaxed when he leaped up onto the jetty and took the line that I passed to him.

I, on the other hand, was not in the least bit relaxed. When Nat helped me climb up onto dry land, my legs were trembling so violently that they would hardly hold me. But they soon got back their strength when Nat put an arm around me and said, "You were great, you know that? I've never had a girl as crew who worked that quickly and well. You'd be fantastic to have as my crew in a yacht race. How about it? I mean, if there are any races before you go home, would you like to crew for me?"

"What about Sandi?" I asked.

"Sandi gets seasick," he said.

I thought about my fear out there and my frozen fingers and the cold water clinging to my jeans.

And then I looked at Nat. "In that case, I'd love to," I said.

"I'm going to get straight into a hot shower when I get home," I said as we walked up the path toward his house.

"Good idea," Nat said, "I don't see the truck, but maybe it's in front of the house, then I can run you up the hill."

The truck was there in the front drive. It was parked next to another car—a small white sports car with the top down. Nat stopped short.

Before he could do anything, the door of the house opened, and the owner of the car came out. I have to say that she was the most gorgeous girl I had ever seen outside of TV commercials. She was wearing tight white jeans that seemed to be part of her body, and her peacock blue sweater really showed off her white-blond hair that fell over her shoulders. Her big blue eyes and button nose—in fact her whole face—were just perfect. She walked quickly down the muddy path toward us like a model on a runway.

"Nat—Nat, honey!" she called, waving wildly to him. "I'm here! I'm finally here."

"What are you doing here?" he asked as we got closer. "I thought you said you were coming tomorrow."

"You don't sound very pleased to see me," she said, pouting. "And after I drove all that way alone, just to be with you—because I couldn't bear to wait any longer."

"Of course I'm pleased to see you," he said softly. He ran the last couple of steps toward her.

"You are a very naughty boy," she said, gazing up into his eyes. "I was worried sick when they told me you had the boat out on a day like this. Goodness, you look a mess! I'm not going to give you your hello kiss till you get cleaned up."

Nat ignored the comment about the kiss.

"What's wrong with today? It was a great day for a sail, wasn't it, Meredith?"

He turned and looked back at me. Sandi seemed to notice for the first time that I was there. She looked me up and down as if I were Exhibit A in the courtroom.

"Who is this, Nat?" she asked in a cool voice. "I don't think I've met her before."

"No, you haven't," Nat said, walking back down the path toward me. "This is Meredith Markham, Sandi."

"Hello, Meredith Markham," Sandi said, coming up to join us, her head held high. "I'm Sandi Cabot. I expect you've heard about me." And she flashed me a smile that showed hundreds of even white teeth but somehow didn't manage to reach her eyes. "Do you live around here?" she asked, and I noticed the sharp edge to her voice.

"No, I'm just visiting for the summer," I said.

I saw the relief cross her face. "Oh. How nice," she said. "Well, I'm glad my Nat's finally found someone crazy enough to ride in that horrible boat with him. I don't know how anyone can enjoy getting cold and wet and dirty. You both look like drowned rats. Now come in the house right away and get into some decent clothes," she said to Nat, grabbing his hand and starting to pull him up the path toward the house.

"Hey, wait a minute, Sandi," Nat said. "I have to drive Meredith home first."

Sandi turned her gaze back to me. I guess I must have looked pretty pathetic standing there shivering with my jeans clinging to me and my hair plastered to my face.

"It's OK," I said bravely. "It's not far. I can walk."

"No, I'll get the truck," Nat said, but Sandi tugged at his hand.

"She says she can walk, Nat," she said firmly. "And I haven't seen you for such a long time—come on. Don't be mean." And she dragged him toward the house.

"Meredith, will you be all right?" he asked, turning back to look at me standing there.

"I'll be fine," I said, starting to walk away.

"Bye Meredith. Nice meeting you. See you again some time," Sandi called sweetly.

Then she shut the door.

I turned away and began to walk home along the road, past the field. Was it the same field that Nat and I had run through, hand in hand, only a few short hours before? It didn't seem possible. It seemed that the boat and the island had all happened in a dream or in another life.

I heard the crunch of gravel as a truck came to a halt beside me. My heart leaped. So Nat had come after me; he had left Sandi and come! I looked over my shoulder and saw a milk truck with Aileen grinning down at me from the front seat.

"You look like you could use a ride," she said, opening the door for me. I climbed in. "What happened to you?" she asked. "Did you fall in the bay or something?"

"I went out sailing," I said. "It got kind of wet and windy out there."

"You went out with Nat?" she asked.

I nodded bleakly.

"But didn't Sandi just arrive? I could swear I saw her car," Aileen said. She stopped short as she noticed my woeful face. "Me and my big mouth again," she said. "Sandi got here, and now Nat's dumped you, right?"

"That sums it up pretty accurately," I said, trying to stop my voice from quivering.

"That's terrible," she said. "But nobody stands much of a chance when she's around. He just worships the ground she walks on. Isn't she something else?"

"She's something else all right," I growled, giving the phrase a different meaning. Aileen understood and smiled.

"Well, never mind. You can go back to your faithful Peter and forget all about it."

"I don't think I want to forget about it," I said sadly. "I don't think I'll ever forget about it."

Chapter Thirteen

The next week was terrible. I felt like a kid who had had her toys taken away the day after Christmas. Before I met Sandi I had had some hope—I thought there was a chance that Nat might realize that he liked me more than her in the end. But as soon as I saw Sandi, I knew it was hopeless. How could I ever compete with a girl like that? She had everything: she was beautiful, and judging by her car and her clothes, she was rich, and she was very sophisticated. She was already a young woman, while I was still just a girl—a girl from the middle of nowhere at that! And most important of all, she had a hold over Nat so that he trotted behind her like a puppy.

Now I knew that I had never stood a chance. Nat had taken me clam digging and out in the boat because he was a friendly sort of person and he wanted company. He was just showing a tourist around. Maybe he'd even chosen me deliberately because everyone could see that I was no threat to Sandi. And as for those kisses the night of the clambake—well, the moon was shining, and he had told me he was hot-blooded! He would have kissed any girl in those circumstances. I had never meant anything special to him at all. I had to face that now.

Finally, one night when I was alone and Aunt Harriet had gone to bed, I let myself cry. It all seemed so unfair. Nat and I had gotten along so well. Out there on the boat we were a team. We could work together so easily we almost knew what the other was thinking. Now I knew that I'd never join him in a race or in anything else. Sandi would never agree to share him with another girl, and it was easy to see who was the boss in that relationship.

Hurry up and get well again, Aunt Harriet, I thought, so that I can go home. The thought of seeing Nat and Sandi around town together was too painful to bear. I made myself think about Peter and how happy I would be to see him again and how we could pick up where we left off. But somehow I couldn't get myself to believe it.

You can't choose who you fall in love with, I told myself. That's the whole problem.

I knew now that I had never really been in love with Peter. Not the way I was with Nat. I had been flattered that Peter had chosen me out of all the girls he could have had. I had been proud to have a boyfriend when most of my friends didn't, and I had really enjoyed hanging out with a popular group of kids. But as for Peter and me picking up where we had left off—well, I just didn't know anymore if it could ever be the same.

Then the question was solved for me, proving once again what I had always believed— that when one thing goes wrong, everything else starts to go wrong, too! I got a letter from Peter, only the second one he had sent all summer. It was full of talk about the cabin and what fun he and Marnie's family had had there, and then he said:

I have to be honest with you, Meredith, although I really don't want to hurt you. You are a neat girl, and I really enjoyed going with you. But at the cabin I discovered how special Marnie is to me. She's shy, and to

133

start with people don't know what she's really like. But when you get to know her, well, you realize what a great girl she is.

Anyway, I guess she's my girlfriend now. She was very upset about letting you down, but I couldn't pretend I liked one girl best when I really liked another. I hope you don't think we went behind your back or anything. These things just seem to happen. Have fun in New England. See you when you get back.

Love,
Peter

I put the letter down slowly. That's right, I thought, these things just seem to happen. You don't always fall in love with the person you should.

I didn't cry. I didn't even feel like crying. My face felt like a hard mask made of china; it seemed to me that I would never feel any emotion again. Now that the things I had been dreading had actually happened, I didn't feel, or couldn't feel, angry or bitter. Of course, Peter and Marnie couldn't help falling in love. Now I had lost a boyfriend and a best friend as well. It seemed that I had no one.

Aunt Harriet must have been less wrapped up in her books than I thought because she noticed that I was drifting around the house more gloomily than any ghost.

"What's the matter, boy trouble?" she asked me out of the blue one evening.

I looked at her in amazement. I had thought her head was always so full of castles of horror and her poor suffering heroines that she never noticed the world outside.

I nodded.

"Which one?" Aunt Harriet asked. "The one at home you had to phone when you first came, or the one here?"

"Both," I said and heaved a big sigh. "They've both decided at the same time that they don't want me."

"Plenty of other fish in the sea," Aunt Harriet said, watching me pour her evening cup of herb tea that smelled and steamed like witches' brew.

"But I don't want the other fish."

She spooned some honey into the tea and stirred briskly. "Then don't give up hope," she said. "Things have the strangest way of sorting themselves out. I remember my heroine Amanda. Or was it Belinda? Anyway, she was the one who loved the doctor who had treated her when she was poisoned. But he thought she loved Otto, the count. The doctor was going away to leave her with Otto, but then halfway to Canada he realized that Otto was doing the poisoning, and he came back to save her just in time."

I smiled politely. "These things only happen in books. In real life, when you lose a boy he stays lost."

"I wouldn't bet on it," Aunt Harriet said. "Even in real life."

I didn't know what an old lady with her head full of Gothic fantasies knew about real life, but after I'd helped Aunt Harriet to her room, I went to bed strangely comforted.

"Got your storm rations all ready?" Aileen asked when she delivered the milk the next day.

I looked at the deep blue sky and laughed. "What would I need storm rations for?"

"Don't you folks ever watch TV?" she asked, shaking her head in despair. "Tropical storm Cleo is heading this way, due to arrive tomorrow. She's already washed away half of South Carolina and doesn't appear to be getting any weaker as she comes up the coast. So you'd better batten down the hatches, if you don't want to get washed out to sea."

Aileen smiled as she said it and didn't appear to be too worried, but I decided to take some extra Snickers bars, just in case we were cut off for a few days.

"Haven't seen you in a while," Aileen said. "Are you giving everyone in town the cold shoulder?"

"There hasn't been much to come down for," I said. Aileen nodded as if she understood.

"You haven't missed much, that's for sure," Aileen said. "Sandi's been parading up and down Main Street as if she's Miss America."

"If the world was a fair place, she would get swept away by tropical storm Cleo," I said. Aileen giggled.

"That's not very nice," she said, "and you shouldn't be greedy. One boyfriend per person at a time, otherwise there aren't enough to go around for people like me."

I had forgotten that Aileen didn't know that I was now completely without a boyfriend, and I didn't feel in any mood to tell her. I didn't want to talk to anyone about how I felt. In fact, I thought, with some gloomy satisfaction, a hurricane would be very much in harmony with my black mood.

"I'd better go and tell Aunt Harriet about the tropical storm," I said. "Do you think that six Snickers bars will see me through?"

"If you run out, I'll make it up here through

rain and hail, just like the mailmen, bringing my precious load of Snickers bars," Aileen said. "But right now I'd better get going. I've got a lot of deliveries to make before the storm comes tonight."

She gave a friendly wave and climbed back into the big truck, and I went inside to tell Aunt Harriet the news.

"Oh, dear," Aunt Harriet said. "I suppose that is one of the disadvantages of having no radio or TV. One does get cut off from the outside world. Thank heavens Aileen came up here, or we might have gone to bed not knowing."

"She didn't look too worried about it," I said. "And we've had enough storms while I've been here to give us some practice."

"Yes, but not tropical storms!" Aunt Harriet exclaimed. "They're almost as bad as hurricanes."

"I wouldn't have thought you'd get tropical storms this far north," I said. "If I were a tropical storm, I'd freeze to death up here or turn away before I got here."

Aunt Harriet smiled, but she still looked worried. "It's not a thing to take lightly, my girl," she said. "I was in a hurricane once in Florida, and I wouldn't want to go through that again. We must make sure the house is secure."

So I had to spend all day checking windows and doors and putting any objects inside that could be hurled around or plants that might get damaged by the wind. Meanwhile, the sky was still clear, and I couldn't help feeling that this old house had seen some pretty fierce storms in its time and wouldn't mind this one much.

In fact, I was kind of interested in seeing a tropical storm. It would be something exciting to talk about when I got home.

"So, what did you do in New England?"

"Well, actually, I was in tropical storm Cleo."

"Tropical storm Cleo! Wow! What was it like?"

It would make up for the fact that I had never seen a tornado. But even when I'd finished taking in every potted plant and every garden chair, I found it hard to believe that the tropical storm was any more than an exaggerated shower meant to liven up the daily weather report.

Some clouds did appear in the early evening, racing crazily across the sky as if they wanted to outrun the storm. It started to rain around nine o'clock, but it was a gentle sort of rain.

Its rhythmic drumming on the roof put me to sleep around ten.

I woke to the most terrible crash. At first I couldn't remember where I was, and in my half-dream I thought a truck had run into the house. When it came again and the whole house shook, I realized it was a crash of thunder. I got up and felt my way across the room to the window. Outside, the world seemed to have gone crazy. The poor stunted pine trees in the garden were bending and twisting in agony, like terrified people reaching hands to the sky for help. The rain was falling in torrents, and every now and then the wind would hurl sheets of it against the house. And the wind! The wind screamed and whined and howled and growled as if it were alive.

I crept back to my bed and tried to sleep. I pulled the covers over my head as I used to do when I was a little girl. I tried to tell myself that I was safe and warm and snug, but even curled into a tight little ball, I couldn't sleep. The whole house seemed to be protesting— creaking and groaning and shuddering. I wondered about the termites. One of Nat's friends had joked about the house being termite ridden. Was that true, and if so, could the house withstand a wind like this? I had a horrible vision of Nat sifting through the rubble for my body, finding my lifeless hand, and crying, "Oh, Meredith, if only I'd realized sooner!"

But then I couldn't stop Sandi from coming into this terrible fantasy and tapping her foot and saying, "Nat, will you please leave that dirty old rubble alone? And put down that body, you might get germs!"

I sighed and decided to shut out any more thoughts of Nat. It was a long night. How I wished that Mom and Dad were in the room down the hall instead of Aunt Harriet. I remembered how I used to climb into bed with them after a bad dream or if a storm got too loud. This storm had definitely gotten too loud, and there was nobody to run to here. At times the whole house shook. I was almost prepared to run down that hall and snuggle up to Aunt Harriet. Almost, but not quite. She was not the cuddliest person in the world.

Just before dawn I must have drifted off to sleep because when I awoke it was light and quite still. I lay without moving and listened. The only sound I could hear was the pounding of the surf below. The wind had stopped. Then I heard the sound of Aunt Harriet hobbling slowly down the hall.

"How did you weather the storm last night?"

she asked cheerfully, making her way across to my window and peering out. "Or did you sleep through the whole thing?"

"I don't think anyone could have slept through that," I said.

"No, it was pretty fierce, wasn't it?" she said. "I just hope too much damage hasn't been done. I bet there will be quite a few boats lost and roofs blown off. Although we seem to have escaped any major damage up here. Just a few shingles off the roof is all I can see."

I got up and pulled on my robe.

"Oh, and by the way," Aunt Harriet said, "we have a visitor for breakfast."

"Who?"

"Oh, just someone come up to see if we're all right."

I wished I'd had the sense to guess who it was and at least brush my hair first. Nat was sitting at the table drinking tea and looking like an ad for the Save Our Seamen Fund in his big boots and yellow oilskins and hat.

"Oh, hi," I said awkwardly. "I didn't expect to see you."

He smiled at me—a nice, warm, friendly smile—as if he were glad to see me. "My father asked me to come up and make sure the house hadn't blown away during the night," he said.

"It didn't," I said.

"I noticed."

Our eyes held each other's for a moment.

"Was there much damage done in town?" Aunt Harriet asked.

"Not too bad, really," Nat said, helping himself to a bran muffin. "A few sheds blown down and windows broken. It looks like a big mess, but there wasn't any real damage. My family was lucky, I suppose. The only damage to our property was a smashed jetty."

"And what about *Stormy Petrel*?" I asked.

"We put her in the boathouse before the storm; if we hadn't, she would have been matchwood by now. There're quite a few folks who did lose their boats. You'll see plenty of wrecked boats around—oh, and talking of wrecked boats, the big news is that a tanker has gone aground on Gull Island."

"A tanker?" Aunt Harriet said. "Was it carrying oil? Was it damaged?"

"We don't know yet," Nat said. "It's just a rumor right now. The Coast Guard went across to check it out. I suppose they've found out by now if it's breaking up or leaking or anything."

"That would be just terrible," Aunt Harriet

said. "An oil spill on this coast would be disastrous, what with the fisheries and the wildlife."

"You don't need to tell me that," Nat said. "Still, we're just hoping for the best. Well, I'd better be going," he said, jumping up and cramming the rest of the muffin into his mouth. "I have the most exciting day ahead. My dad kindly volunteered me to help with clean-up operations! So he'll be mad if he finds me hiding out up here. See you later, OK?"

He turned and walked toward the door. All I saw of Nat these days, I thought, was his back, disappearing!

"Well, if you need any extra help," Aunt Harriet called after him, "I'm sure Meredith would love to come and lend a hand."

"Thanks," he said, turning back and looking straight at me. "I might take her up on that." Then he hurried out through the front door.

Chapter Fourteen

As soon as Nat had gone and we heard the crunch of his tires on the gravel down below, I turned on Aunt Harriet angrily. "You didn't have to interfere like that," I said. My cheeks were burning with embarrassment and anger.

"Like what, dear?" she asked smoothly.

"You know very well what. Volunteering me to help Nat. He has Sandi to help him, remember?"

"From what I hear, she's not the helping kind," Aunt Harriet said. She smiled at me sweetly, then she slowly hobbled away down the passage.

Of course he won't need me, I said to myself. And what's more, I'm not going to sit here waiting for him. And, what's even more, even if he does ask me, I'm not going to go

145

down there and watch him with Sandi. I can just see her sitting there in her nice white jeans saying, "Oh, Nat, honey, don't get your fingers dirty touching that muddy old wood. Why don't you let what's-her-name pick it up for you?"

I made up my mind I wouldn't even be around the house just in case Nat did come looking for me. I went over to the window and looked out. The sky was still hazy and gray, but rain was only falling in a light mist. I put on Aunt Harriet's big waterproof coat that hung on a hook in the front hall and went out.

Outside, everything was unnaturally still, as if the world were in a state of shock from the violence of the night. Inside, we had heard the wind and rain, but it was impossible to actually realize their strength. In the garden whole beds of flowers were flattened so completely that it looked as if a herd of cattle had run over them. Tree branches lay scattered on the ground. And this was in a walled garden, protected from the full force of the wind!

I opened the gate and walked down to the beach. When I arrived there, I just stood with my mouth open. The beach was so littered it looked like a garbage dump. There was a rowboat with a smashed bottom, patio furniture, a child's sneaker, seaweed and driftwood, dead fish and birds, all piled in horrible heaps. Already it smelled of rot and decay.

I walked along the beach, holding my breath now and then to block out the smell. Then, as I glanced at one heap of junk over beside the water, I thought I saw something move. I was scared to go nearer, but I was curious, too. Step by step I picked my way across the wet sand to get a closer look. When the thing moved again, I jumped. It was a big black bird, lying on its side. I thought for a moment that it was dead and that the movement had just been caused by the wind ruffling its feathers. But then I made myself look closer, and I saw its fierce bright yellow eye looking at me without blinking.

"Poor old thing," I said softly. I tried to identify it from Nat's bird-watching sessions, but I had never seen any bird that was big and black like that one. I knelt down beside it. It moved its head in alarm as I came near, and as it did I saw a spot of purest white.

Suddenly I realized. The bird wasn't black at all. It was a big white herring gull, and it was covered in oil.

That tanker! I thought. It was carrying oil, and it did spill some! I looked at the bird with its horrible, gooey, black body and I felt sick.

He's bound to die soon, there's nothing you can do for him anyway, the coward in me whispered. There must be hundreds of dead birds lying along the shore after the storm.

I tried to walk away. But I couldn't just leave him. That golden eye seemed to follow my every movement.

I'll go into town, I decided, and tell someone there. The police and firemen will know what to do.

I watched a wave come rushing up the shore. It hissed over the wet sand and came toward my feet. The next wave came even closer. Oh no, I thought. The tide's coming in! Now what do I do? The water had almost reached the bird. OK, I decided, or rather the braver part of me did, I'd better move it back a bit and leave it higher up the beach.

I stood there and looked at it. It looked at me. Go on, pick it up, I commanded myself, but my fingers shrank from touching that gooey mess and getting near that fierce beak.

I think I'd better mention that I am not exactly used to dealing with wild animals. The only pet our family ever owned was an old cat who spent all day lying in the sun. He was so gentle I used to push him around in my doll carriage. My only experiences with animals were with that cat and Marnie's parakeet—and the parakeet always stayed safely in his cage! Hardly enough training for picking up large, fierce-looking, wounded sea gulls!

Then the next wave broke with some force and came rushing up, almost to my feet. Then I realized I had better do something fast.

I moved toward the bird as he lifted his head and turned that beak nearer to my fingers. I moved my hand back seconds before the beak struck.

"Listen here, bird," I said. "We are not doing a scene out of *The Birds*, do you understand? If you want to be rescued, you've got to do what you're told."

But that eye still looked fierce and not at all compliant.

When a wave rushed right up to the gull, he tried to get up, helplessly flapping his heavy, oil-laden wings. He was obviously exhausted already. In desperation I grabbed an old piece of canvas that looked as if it had been a part of a beach umbrella, flung it around the gull, and picked it up quickly. It was much lighter than I had expected and came flying up into my arms, making me stagger over a pile of junk like a drunkard.

It was at that moment, staggering with an oily bird and trying not to get pecked or covered in oil, that I saw a car screech to a halt on the road. It was Sandi's white sports car. Nat jumped out of the passenger seat and came running down the gently sloping hillside.

"Meredith, what are you doing?" he yelled.

I no longer cared if he was Nat or King Kong. I was just glad to see him and to get some help.

"This gull is covered in oil," I yelled back. "The tide is coming in, so I have to bring him farther up on the beach."

Nat climbed over the debris to my side. "Let me see," he said, calmly taking the bird from me. "Oh, the poor thing." The gull didn't attempt to struggle but lay quietly in his arms while he stroked its head. "That makes me so mad," he said. "You should hear what they're saying in town—nothing to worry about, only a minor spill, and it's all contained, and it isn't coming in this direction anyway. But it's quite obvious it must have reached some of the islands. I wonder how many other birds we'll find in this condition."

The car horn blared out and made the bird struggle again so that Nat almost dropped him.

"Come on, honey," Sandi called. "What are

you doing? Your dad said we don't have much time before you have to help out in town."

Nat turned to me. "I'd better get this bird back to my house and try and clean it up," he said. He walked back toward the car.

So that's that, I thought in disappointment. Nat and Sandi drive off into the sunset, leaving the real heroine all alone again!

"What on earth have you got there?" Sandi asked, standing up and peering over the top of the MG.

"It's a gull, and I've got to get it back home quickly and clean it up," Nat answered calmly.

When Sandi spoke she didn't sound at all calm. In fact, she sounded one step away from hysterical. "Oh, Nat, please don't bring it near me," she said, shuddering. "You know I don't like things like that!"

"Nobody likes it, Sandi," Nat said. "Least of all the gull. Look at the poor thing. We've got to get it back quickly, or it'll die."

"Nat, I won't have that disgusting thing in my car," Sandi said, her voice rising.

"Come on, Sandi," Nat said with urgency, "it's just around the curve, and I'll keep it away from the upholstery."

"Nat, it's covered in oil!" Sandi shrieked. "It's going to flap its wings and panic and cover everything. I won't have it in the car!

You said yourself it's not far—" Her gaze went across to me. "Look, you've got a willing little helper here, let her carry it, and we'll meet her down at the house."

"Sandi!" Nat said angrily.

"Are you coming or aren't you?" Sandi asked. Then, without waiting for a reply, she gunned the engine and was gone.

Nat and I stood looking after her. I think we were both equally amazed.

"Sandi is not very good in a crisis," he said, looking embarrassed. He started off down the road toward his house, the gull in his arms. "Are you coming?" he called after me.

Sandi's description of me as the willing little helper still stung.

"You can manage perfectly well without me, I guess," I said stiffly.

"Well, if you're busy—" he said hesitantly, but his eyes pleaded. "I really could do with someone to hold the bird while I clean it. Someone who won't panic."

Of course I gave in. Probably a big mistake, I thought. Probably I'll be hurt and humiliated again when Sandi comes to claim him afterward. But I couldn't resist those eyes. Also, I didn't want that poor gull to die after all my efforts.

Together we trudged down the road to Nat's

house. The distance seemed to have doubled, and I was glad it was Nat carrying the bird and not me. Once I did offer to take it from him, but he just smiled and said he was OK. We were almost there when a pickup screeched to a halt beside us. The driver was Robbie. "We've been looking all over for you," he called to Nat. "You're needed badly. We figured you'd know what to do. I see you've got another one there."

"Another what?"

"Bird. People keep bringing in these poor birds covered in oil. They say there're whole beaches full of them. We've called for the humane society officer, but I guess he's busy. You're the only other person who knows anything about birds. Come on, jump in, and let's get going."

"Climb up, Meredith," Nat said. I scrambled up into the truck, and then I helped Nat with the sea gull. The gull, who had been lying quietly in his arms, began to panic again when it heard the noise of the truck.

"Stupid bird," Robbie said, trying to avoid the oil-covered wings. "They're all like that—squawking and struggling. You'd think the poor things would know we want to help them."

"Where have you got them?" Nat asked,

managing to subdue the gull again so that it just gave a halfhearted squawk every now and then.

"We've put them in the kindergarten playground," Robbie said. "We figured that was the one fenced-in area that's close to everything."

We drove into town and finally turned into the schoolyard. It looked like a battle area—and sounded like one, too. People were rushing around, and birds were screaming. The honks and squawks and cries were surely noisier than the kindergarten class when it was in residence.

"Oh, there's Nat now. Ask him," a voice called.

"Thank goodness you're here," a woman said. "What are we supposed to do with these birds? I can't see that we'll ever get this oil off. It's just hopeless."

Nat was already stripping off his jacket and rolling up his sleeves. "You need lots of tubs of warm water," he said. "And as many old towels and sheets as possible—oh, and dish-washing liquid."

"Dish-washing liquid?" someone asked.

"That's the best thing," Nat said. "It's mild enough so that it doesn't hurt them. Make sure you bring a mild one, you know—softens-your-hands-while-you-do-the-dishes—or something like that."

Under Nat's direction people filled tubs with warm water. Then he showed them how to gently rub the liquid soap into the oily feathers, rinse it off in the tub, then repeat it in tub after tub until the feathers came clean.

Of course, on paper it sounds very easy. But it wasn't. For one thing, the least affected birds, those we really should have been able to help, struggled and made tremendous fusses so that we ended up with more soapy water on us than on them. Then there was always the problem of their catching cold. Nat told us that this was one of the biggest dangers, so we had to make sure they didn't get chilled between tubs and that they were dried well afterward and put into a warm room to recover. The janitor's room was taken over for that purpose. We thought it might be asking a bit much to let birds fly all over the kindergarten classroom!

I held the birds while Nat cleaned them, and we all worked very efficiently. We were just finishing up and telling ourselves what a good job we had done when a truck pulled in with another whole load; all the birds in this new batch were badly covered.

We tried hard, but the soapy water just

wasn't enough for these gulls. In the end we had to use mineral oil, and we weren't too hopeful that the birds would survive. A lot of them seemed to be badly shocked from the oil and the truck ride, and many just collapsed pathetically as we finished with them.

No one was more glad than I was to see the humane society officer finally arrive. I had this wonderful feeling that he would say, "You've all done fine jobs, but I'll take over now." Instead of that, he stepped from his truck, looked around, and said, "Well, you seem to know what you're doing here, so I'll leave you to it. They've been yelling for me to get over to Littlehampton. No one has a clue of what to do with the gulls over there, by the sound of it, and they're in a real mess—oil all over the beaches." Then before anyone could stop him, he climbed back into his truck again and was off.

We worked on. After a couple of hours, I no longer remembered that I was scared of touching wild birds or scared of getting pecked. I had gotten pecked and clawed so many times that day that I didn't even notice it anymore. Our clothes seemed to have more oil on them than the birds. Even my hair felt heavy and sticky with oil.

It seemed as if it would never end. Just

when we thought we were finishing up, more birds would be brought in, each batch in worse shape than the one before. Nat's mother came over from the restaurant with soup and sandwiches for everyone.

"Oh, so you're Meredith," she said as she fed me a sandwich—my hands were too dirty to think of touching food! "Nat's done nothing but talk about you."

That remark made me feel ready to tackle a few oil-covered ostriches.

The cleaning of each bird was a long, painstaking job, and the ones that were not too far gone into exhaustion fought us all the way. Nat told us that we had to work as quickly as possible because if we didn't, the birds would start to clean themselves, swallow oil, and die. That fact was enough to prevent anyone from sneaking a quick rest.

I was concentrating so hard that I didn't have time to notice anything around me. I was very surprised when I finally looked up and saw that it was getting dark.

"I really ought to go home," I told Nat. "My aunt will wonder what's happened to me."

"Don't go," Nat pleaded. "You're the best person we've got. Let me send someone up with a message for your aunt."

So I stayed. Nat's mother appeared again

with supper, but I was so tired and busy that I don't even remember eating it. Just before night fell, the sky cleared, and the setting sun lit up the whole scene in glorious orange and pink color.

As if on cue, Sandi arrived. Stepping out of her sports car, dressed in a deep orange satin jumpsuit that matched the sky, with the sun shining on her wonderful gold hair, she looked like a fairy princess come down among the goblins.

"Nat, honey," she called in a silky voice. "I've come to get you. You've done enough. Let's go."

Nat looked up from the grebe we were both working on and frowned.

"You can see I'm busy," he said.

"Let somebody else do it now," Sandi pleaded. "You've really done your share."

"There is nobody else, Sandi," he said shortly. "That should be quite obvious. Why don't you go home and get changed into some old clothes, then come and join us? We need every pair of hands we can get. If these birds don't get help soon, they'll all die."

Sandi looked amused and horrified at the same time, as if he were suggesting that she start taming lions.

"I'm afraid that sort of thing is not my bag,

honey," she said. "You know how I hate getting dirty."

"Then go away and leave us in peace," Nat snapped.

Sandi looked surprised and hurt. "But, Nat, you remember how you promised to drive me over to Portland for dinner tonight," she said, pouting like a five-year-old. "I'm all dressed and ready. Don't say you're going to let me down."

"I'm not going anywhere tonight, Sandi," Nat said, not even looking at her. "You've got to learn you can't always have your own way."

"If you can't take me, I'll just have to find someone who can," Sandi said.

"Then that's what you'd better do, find someone else," Nat answered, while he continued to work on the grebe.

"OK. I'll do it," she said icily and began to pick her way across the mud back to her car.

"In which case don't bother to come back," he called after her.

The car door slammed. She drove away so violently that the tires screamed on the pavement.

I tried not to look at Nat. I kept right on working. As I worked an amazing thought struck me. I thought that I might have turned out just like Sandi. As I'd watched her standing there in her orange satin jumpsuit, so out of place in the mud and grime, I realized that I *had* been very like her—caring more about how I looked than about anything else. I had grown up a lot in a few weeks. In the end, whatever happened between Nat and me, I had learned a lot from him.

Chapter Fifteen

Nat and I worked on in silence. Night fell. Someone brought in a spotlight from the auto shop, and we kept working. My whole body ached with tiredness. When the sun set, a cold wind had sprung up, and my hands and feet felt cold and wet and miserable. I felt that if anyone said "boo" to me I would burst into tears. But I didn't let Nat see how I was feeling, and I kept working. There was no question of quitting; someone had to finish cleaning the birds, and that someone was me.

As it got later, more and more people drifted away until there were only a handful of us left. Apart from things like, "Here, hand me that towel," and "Watch it, hold its beak!" we didn't say anything to each other.

I began to slip beyond tiredness. My body responded as if it were only programmed to pick up birds, clean them, and put them down again.

Then at last I picked up a tiny, bedraggled thing, too oil-covered to be recognizable. As I cleaned away, I saw a brilliant flash of red and then of metallic green.

"Oh, Nat," I called. "Come and look at this. What is it?"

He came over. "Oh, what a beautiful little duck," he said. "And what a mess it's in. Go very gently with it, it's so small."

"I wish the ASPCA man would come and take over with this one," I said. "Or you, could you do it for me?"

"You'll do just as well as I could, if not better," Nat said. "You're so gentle with them, and they're not scared of you."

I knew it was a compliment, but I was too tired and too strained to smile. I just carried the duck across to the first tub of warm water and began sponging. I worked slowly, almost one feather at a time, stopping to cover the little body in a towel when the wind blew too cold. At last his pretty little head was completely clean, and I could see the lovely streak of red behind the bill, the fine line of black dots on white, and the incredible little

162

white crown. He was the most beautiful bird we had seen all day.

"There!" I said in triumph at last. "I think I've done it. He looks like a real bird again, doesn't he?"

But as I picked him up to carry him across to the recovery area, that beautiful head suddenly fell back, and he was dead.

Tears started to sting in my eyes. I fought them back. "No," I pleaded. "Don't die now. Please, don't die." I stroked the limp little body, trying to will it back to life.

"How's it going?" Nat asked cheerfully as he came across to me.

I put the bird down on the tabletop. "It was all for nothing," I tried to say in a calm, even voice. "It died anyway." Then I burst into sobs.

Nat didn't say anything. He simply drew me to him and held me tightly.

"It's just not fair," I said, sobbing onto his shoulder. "We worked so hard. We tried so hard. It's not fair that this little duckling had to die. Has everything we've been doing all been for nothing?"

"It's OK," he said, stroking my hair as if I were a little girl. "Go ahead and cry. You'll feel much better afterward."

I don't know how long we stood there, but I

do know that I made his shoulder pretty we
and he didn't complain.

"I'm OK now," I said, trying to brush the
tears away. "I suppose we'd better get back to
work."

Nat let go of me slowly. "Meredith, it's no
for nothing, you know," he said. "We knew
from the start that the survival rate is not too
high. It never is with birds. They go into shock
too easily. But even if we can save only a few
of them, in the end, it has to be worth it
doesn't it? And it's better for them to di
here than to slowly drown or die of starvation
because they can't feed, or be attacked by dog.
because they can't fly away. Even if we could
only save one, I think it would be worth it
Now come on," he said, taking my hand as i
I were one of the kindergartners who usuall
played there. "I'm taking you home."

"But I can't leave before we're finished,"
said, sobbing. "There's still so much more t
do."

"You have worked over and above the ca
of duty," he said firmly. "And I am personall
ordering you to quit."

He walked me over to his father's truck
and we rode all the way back with his arr
around me.

"Look," he said, giving me a little smile, "it's almost day."

The first pale greenish streaks were appearing out across the ocean. Nat pulled up below Stormhaven.

"Meredith," he said, stroking my hair back from my face, "I can't tell you how wonderful you were. You are the only girl I've ever met who could do what you've done. You didn't panic, you didn't complain, you didn't make any excuses to get out of it, you just kept on going—"

"I know," I said—a little too sharply, I think. "I'm wonderful in a crisis. Just like one of the boys."

"Not at all like one of the boys. And let me tell you something—I was really glad when you started to cry down there. I was kind of worried about you before. I began to wonder if I'd gotten myself mixed up with the Iron Maiden—you know—someone who wasn't scared out in the boat in that storm, not scared of picking up all those birds. It's nice to know that you really are human after all, because I don't want to be in love with a robot."

A robot? I thought. If only he could have seen the trembling hands and the knocking knees. Then I realized he had said he was in love with me. I had to ask him. I couldn't let it pass.

"But what about Sandi?" I said aloud. "Won't she be back to claim you as soon as you're all cleaned up and presentable again?"

"I'm no longer available to be claimed."

"She's been your girl for a long time. Are you just going to give her up over a little thing like this?"

"Sandi was a habit, I guess," he said. "A very expensive habit, too. But all habits can be broken, can't they?"

"I guess so," I said. "I hope so."

"Well, I'm breaking one right now," he said.

Then his arms went around me, and his lips found mine. And suddenly every bit of the coldness and the tiredness just melted away, and not even Sandi mattered anymore.

Chapter Sixteen

"For someone who's supposed to be taking care of her disabled aunt, you certainly aren't around much these days," Aunt Harriet said at breakfast one morning.

"I'm sorry," I said, feeling a bit guilty. "It's just that since Nat—"

She smiled. "I understand. I was only teasing you. You've taken care of me splendidly, and I'm really delighted everything is working out so well for you. Is Nat taking you to the dance on Saturday?"

"Yes, he is. How did you know?"

"I have my spies. To be more accurate, Aileen brought up the groceries yesterday while you were out in that awful boat again. She tells me that this dance is *the* big social event of the year around here. You'll even have to wear something special. There's a nice little dress boutique in Littlehampton. Why don't you get Nat to drive you over there?"

"Aunt Harriet, there's a slight question of cash. Boutiques are never exactly cheap."

"If you hadn't frittered away your allowance on Snickers bars—" She laughed.

"How did you know about the Snickers bars?" I asked, aghast.

"I'm not blind, you know! I've noticed the wrappers in your room. And those onion-and-garlic potato chips on your breath!" Aunt Harriet laughed some more, then she said, "Actually, you didn't let me finish. I was going to say that you might need this," and she held out a fifty-dollar bill.

"But, Aunt Harriet, I couldn't take that."

"Don't be silly. If you hadn't come, I'd have had to pay a live-in nurse, and just think how much that would have cost me! So this is just some of the money you've saved me."

I went over and hugged her. "Aunt Harriet, you really are a nice lady," I said.

"Has it taken you this long to discover that?" she asked with a little smile.

The dress was a dream. As soon as I saw it hanging in the little store called Shorebirds, I knew I had to have it. It had a dark blue, full, pleated skirt, covered with tiny white flowers and a white lacy top with ribbons. It looked like something a girl from a hundred years ago would have worn. If anyone at home had told me that I would wear a dress like that, I would have told them they were crazy. But here it seemed just right, especially since I was going to a dance with a boy from two hundred years ago.

Nat obviously thought it looked just right, too, when he came to pick me up. He gave me a big beaming smile and spun me around so he could admire me from all directions.

"If I were from somewhere else in the country, I would probably say, 'Wow, you look absolutely fantastic,' " he said. "But since I'm a typical New Englander, I'll just have to say, 'Mmm. Not bad at all.' "

"Well, I'm glad to see you're not wearing sea boots," I quipped back.

"I have them in the car in case I need some assistance with my dancing," he said with a straight face.

"Take care of her, Nat," Aunt Harriet called.

"Don't worry. I'll watch over her like her guardian angel," Nat called back. "I need her to crew for me in the race next week."

Then he waved and dragged me down the steps at a run.

The dance was something I never would have gone to at home. Until then I had believed that only sophisticated things could be fun for mature people like me. I wouldn't have been caught dead inside a community center decorated like a barn with big bales of hay for seats and a country-and-western band. But the thing that struck me as soon as we opened the door was that all the kids really seemed to be having fun. Of course, there were one or two kids who sat on hay bales and looked wistfully at each couple that danced past. But the faces of most of the people were full of laughter. That certainly wasn't the way it was at the discos I went to. There, psychedelic lights flashed, the music was loud enough to split eardrums, and each dancer looked as if he or she were locked into an individual time capsule.

When I saw the country-and-western theme of the dance, I was scared that I wouldn't know any of the steps. But the band was great and played everything from slow numbers to cotton-eyed joe, and even I picked that one up quickly. But I liked the slow numbers best.

About mid-evening, when we had just settled down on a bale of hay with cool drinks, I felt Nat become tense beside me. I looked up, and there in the doorway was Sandi. Sandi, looking more lovely than ever, if that was possible. She was wearing a long, white strapless dress, which showed off her golden tan, and she had tucked a white gardenia behind one ear. Next to all the kids in their country clothes, she looked like a rose in a garden of dandelions. Her cool gaze swept over the dance floor, picking out her target.

Then she saw Nat and began to walk right across the middle of the floor, not seeming to notice the dancers who had to swerve out of her way.

When she was only a few feet away from us, she cooed, "Hi, Nat," in her soft, low voice.

"Hello, Sandi," he said flatly.

"I didn't think you'd dare to come here without me," she said. "Seeing that this has always been *our* special dance."

"I came with Meredith," Nat said in the same even voice. "You remember Meredith, the one who stuck with me to clean all those birds and didn't go running off like a spoiled brat?"

Her gaze was cold as she looked at me, like a snake does when it's sizing up its next victim. "Ah, yes, Meredith," she said. "I must say it's the first time I've seen you not looking like a drowned rat."

"What do you want, Sandi?" Nat asked sharply.

"What a silly question," she said, smiling to show all those lovely teeth. "You, of course. I want to talk to you."

"Not now," Nat said.

"Now or never," Sandi replied.

There was a pause. Even the music seemed to stop.

"All right. Let's go outside then," Nat said, getting up slowly. He touched my shoulder. "I'll be right back," he told me.

As I watched the two of them disappear through the big double doors, I couldn't help feeling uneasy. No, it was more than that—I felt downright scared. Although I had heard the coolness in Nat's voice, I couldn't help worrying. After all, she was so lovely, so smooth, so sophisticated—in short, she was everything I had dreamed of being and had tried to be—once. The funny thing was that I didn't want to be that way anymore. I knew now that there was more to life than looking like Cheryl Tiegs and wanting expensive clothes and being bored with everything. Life was meant to be fun, and I, for one, was going to have fun from now on. I was going to crew in Nat's race the next week. Then, when I got home, I was going to try and join a sailing club there. I was going to get involved with things at school—maybe try out for a play or join the volleyball team. But I was going to have fun with a capital F, whatever happened.

I knew that I didn't want to be like Sandi, but I also knew that a girl like her was the superdeluxe model and could easily turn a boy's head.

As the minutes slipped away, I began to feel more and more uneasy. I found myself staring at those doors as if I were willing Nat to come back right then. She couldn't have persuaded him to go with her, could she? He couldn't have driven off with her and just left me there alone. He wouldn't expect me to find my own way home, would he? I didn't know anymore. Part of me said that I trusted Nat completely, that he wouldn't let me down. The other part reminded me that he had admitted that Sandi was a habit, one he was going to break. I remembered that that was what my father had said once about cigarette smoking. Then a few weeks later he had taken it up again.

So I sat there alone, swishing the ice cubes in the bottom of my drink, trying to look cool

173

and occupied and not in the least worried that my date had left twenty minutes before with a gorgeous, rich, and spoiled girl who always got her own way.

When I felt a tap on my shoulder, I looked up, expecting it to be Nat. But it was only Robbie.

"Want to dance?" he asked.

"Sure, why not?" I said, taking his hand. After all, it was better than sitting by myself.

Robbie must have known that Nat had left with Sandi, but he was kind enough not to mention it. He hardly talked at all. Only once, when I guess I glanced toward the door for the hundredth time, he said in a low voice, "Don't worry, he'll be back."

But I did worry. The set of dances finished, and the band took a break. Robbie brought me another cup of punch, and I was glad to have something to sip again. At least I looked occupied. I began to sink into deeper and deeper gloom. Nat had been gone so long that even if he did come back, it would just be to tell me that he and Sandi had made up again and he didn't want me anymore.

But I was trapped there, and somehow I had to find someone to give me a ride home.

The music began again with a rock number, and a strange boy asked me to dance. The whole scene began to take on an unreal quality, as in a nightmare. I felt trapped by the throb of the music and the wild movement all around me. Then suddenly, through my nightmare, a voice was saying, "Mind if I cut in on this one? You're dancing with my girl."

My partner melted away, and in his place was Nat, smiling at me as if nothing were wrong in the whole world.

"What happened to Sandi?" I asked.

"Can't hear you," he mouthed back. "Let's go outside where it's not so loud."

We fought our way through the jungle of couples. Outside it was calm and clear. Stars hung above our heads like diamonds. The ocean murmured in the distance.

"So, where's Sandi?" I asked again.

"Gone, never to return," he said and grinned.

"You were away so long."

"You didn't look like you were missing me too much," he said. "I was pretty jealous when I came in and saw you dancing. That guy you were with is the most popular guy in Littlehampton!"

"I had to do something to pass the time," I said. "I thought you'd abandoned me."

"I'd never do that," he said seriously. "Did you really think I wouldn't come back?"

"Well, you were away so long—and she looked so fantastic—"

"It's over, Meredith," he said simply. "I'm sorry it took a long time, but, well, we had a bit of an ugly scene. She threw a tantrum. She always does when she can't get her own way. So I thought it was best to calm her down and convince her to drive home before she came back in here and embarrassed you, too. You have to understand, it's not easy for her, being the only child in her family. Her parents really spoil her. She's always got what she wanted as soon as she wanted it. You can't help growing up badly when you're treated like that."

"So, why did you go with her for so long?"

"I told you, she was a habit. At first, when I was only a freshman, I was flattered that such a great-looking girl was interested in me. It was a real status thing around here to have a girl like that. Besides, the first year she tried really hard to be nice. But it's been getting worse for the past three years. In the end I couldn't stand being treated like her pet dog anymore. I told her that. She's going back to Boston in the morning. I guess her parents will stay up here for the rest of the summer; they've got a live-in maid at home, so Sandi won't be alone."

"Oh," I said. I didn't know what else to say.

"And you and I," Nat said, "are going to have a great time for the next couple of months, winning every yacht race on the coast!"

Chapter Seventeen

We did just that! If I had thought plain sailing was exciting, it was nothing compared to racing. Nat was a strict teacher and made me practice with him for hours every day. In the end we didn't have to talk to each other at all. We knew just what the other was thinking, which was useful when we couldn't make our voices heard above the noise of the wind.

When we won our first race, I felt as if I'd won the Olympics. I put everything else out of my mind except Nat and sailing. All I thought of was what time I would see Nat the next day and what race was coming up on the weekend. There was no more Chicago, no more Peter nor Marnie, nor even Kelly the lifeguard.

That's why it came as a big shock when Aunt Harriet said one morning, "Meredith, would you please ask Sam to have the taxi here at eight tomorrow morning?"

"What for? Is something wrong?"

"No, nothing's wrong. Quite the opposite. Tomorrow is the big day when I finally have my cast taken off. Freedom again! Won't that be marvelous? No more asking you to run down and get my natural foods for me."

"That's great, Aunt Harriet," I said, trying to sound as though I meant it. "But you'll still need someone to help you for a while, won't you?"

"My dear child, I won't even be here after next week," Aunt Harriet said. "I have my writers' conference to attend in Texas. I was so worried my leg wouldn't heal in time for me to go. I always look forward to the conference so much. Gothic Writers of America—we all get together and scare each other to death!" She laughed so happily that I tried hard to be glad for her and not to think that it was the end of the world for me.

"I suppose you wouldn't want me to stay on and keep up the house for you while you're away, would you?" I asked.

She smiled as if she understood. "I'm afraid not, Meredith. You see I only rented this house for the summer. I won't be coming back here after the conference. I'll be going straight back to my apartment in New York. And you—well, your family will want to see something of you, and you'll have to start thinking about school again soon. And, Meredith, I think we'll arrange for you to take the train this time. It'll be a nice ride, and you'll get to see some of the country. Now won't that be fun?"

"I suppose so," I said hesitantly.

She came over and put an arm around me. "I know it's hard to say goodbye," she said. "But there will be a lot of goodbyes while you're growing up. It's something you'll have to get used to."

I felt a tear begining to creep down my cheek. "But at least I can stay for the race on Saturday, can't I?" I said. I must have sounded like a two-year-old. "Nat and I have been practicing hard to win the silver cup—"

Aunt Harriet couldn't help smiling. "Of course, you can stay until Saturday," she said.

The race went splendidly. It was a perfect day: clear sky, stiff breeze, white spray. And because I knew it was going to be the last race with Nat, I made sure I imprinted every detail of it in my memory. I knew I could never forget the sting of spray in my face, the taste of salt on my lips, and Nat sitting there looking serious and excited at the same time. I would remember forever the way our arch-rival boat, *Miss Suzy*, had gradually pulled ahead of us and then how we did a supertight turn and cut through on the inside to win.

I thought about it again as we waited at the train depot on a gray Monday morning. That day there was no breeze, and the sky was heavy with the promise of rain. It matched my mood perfectly, but I tried to be cheerful as Nat stood beside me, holding my hand.

"Maybe by next year I'll be so good that you'll have to crew for me," I quipped as I watched the sleek, powerful monster of a train creep into the station and stop with a sigh. Doors opened and slammed. People hurried. It's here, I thought. The train that's going to take me home—back to Marnie and Peter and the life I have always taken for granted, but which will never be the same again.

"I'm not going to promise to write to you," Nat said, "because I'm not great at writing letters to start with—and besides, romances don't really work out long distance. We're both going to change a lot and date other people. If we meet again, we might be disappointed that we had changed. So let's just remember this summer and the great times we had together, OK?"

"I guess you're right," I said in a wobbly voice. Luckily we had both had some experience with romances carried on long distance. I could remember how disappointed I was by Peter's letters, and Nat knew all about Sandi's changing. It wouldn't have been right to put each other through that.

Down the platform someone was blowing a whistle.

"I'd better not get left behind," I said.

"Hey, don't look so sad," Nat said, stroking my cheek. "Just think that one day you'll be able to tell your grandchildren: 'When I was sixteen I met the most amazingly good-looking, talented boy, and we had a perfect summer together.' "

I laughed through my tears as I climbed up into the train. The door slammed behind me. With a jerk and a wheeze we started to move forward.

Aunt Harriet, standing on two good legs, waved from the background. Nat stood there, his hair blowing in the wind, looking exactly like the ghost I had met so long ago. He didn't wave, he just watched me go. I realized then that saying goodbye was not easy for him, either.

I sat back in my seat and watched, unseeing, as green countryside flashed past. When I was sixteen, I thought, I met the most amazingly good-looking, talented boy, and we had a perfect summer together. That's just what I would tell my grandchildren.

Don't miss any of these great new
Sweet Dreams romances, on sale soon!

☐ **#55 SPOTLIGHT ON LOVE by Nancy Pines (On sale January 15, 1984 • 23964-3 • $1.95)**
—After sticking to a strict diet all summer, Callie's dream has come true. She's slender, attractive—and up for the romantic lead in the school musical opposite handsome David Palmer. He makes her heart do flip-flops, and, to her amazement, seems to like her too. But Callie's visions of a long-running romance are shattered when Kim Crawford comes on the scene. Will Callie find herself out of the spotlight while Kim and David take center stage?

☐ **#56 CAMPFIRE NIGHTS by Dale Cowan (On sale January 15, 1984 • 23965-1 • $1.95)**
—Jill's summer as a junior counselor starts off with a bang when Brad Cassidy, the gorgeous new waterfront counselor, begins paying attention to her. She's on cloud nine—despite the fact that she doesn't really trust him. Then Jill meets quiet, serious Skip, and they spend hours just walking and talking. But somehow, Skip's just not as exciting as Brad. . . .

□ **#57 ON HER OWN by Suzanne Rand (On sale February 15, 1984 • 23966-X • $1.95)**
—Most of the kids in the Roughing It program seem to have had a lot more experience with the Adirondack wilderness than Katie. But Lisa, who's become Katie's instant best friend, is more than willing to lend her a hand—until Jake Summers begins to take an interest in Katie. Katie's crazy about Jake, too—but he's Lisa's old boyfriend . . . and she's still in love with him.

□ **#58 RHYTHM OF LOVE by Stephanie Foster (On sale February 15, 1984 • 23970-8 • $1.95)**
—Darcy lost the two most important things in her life the day Scott told her he didn't need her as a keyboard player anymore—the fun of being in his band, and the chance to be his girlfriend. So she decides to get his attention by forming her own group . . . and that's when her troubles really start!

Buy these books at your local bookstore or use this handy coupon for ordering:

Bantam Books, Inc., Dept. SD4, 414 East Golf Road, Des Plaines, Ill. 60016

Please send me the books I have checked above. I am enclosing $_____ (please add $1.25 to cover postage and handling. Send check or money order—no cash or C.O.D.'s please).

Mr/Ms _____

Address_____

City/State _____ Zip _____

SD4—1/84

Please allow four to six weeks for delivery. This offer expires 7/84. Prices and availability subject to change without notice.

SPECIAL MONEY SAVING OFFER

Now you can have an up-to-date listing of Bantam's hundreds of titles plus take advantage of our unique and exciting bonus book offer. A special offer which gives you the opportunity to purchase a Bantam book for only 50¢. Here's how!

By ordering any five books at the regular price per order, you can also choose any other single book in the catalog (up to a $4.95 value) for just 50¢. Some restrictions do apply, but for further details why not send for Bantam's illustrated Shop-At-Home Catalog today!

Just send us your name and address plus 50¢ to defray the postage and handling costs.

BANTAM BOOKS, INC.
Dept. FC, 414 East Golf Road, Des Plaines, Ill. 60016

Mr./Mrs./Miss/Ms. _____
(please print)

Address _____

City _____ State _____ Zip _____

FC—12/83